D1024993

MARVEL

MARVEL ACTION

AVENGERS

THE NEW DANGER

Marvel Publishing:

Jeff Youngquist: VP Production & Special Projects
Caitlin O'Connell: Assistant Editor, Special Projects
Sven Larsen: Director, Licensed Publishing
David Gabriel: SVP Print, Sales & Marketing
C.B. Cebulski: Editor In Chief
Joe Quesada: Chief Creative Officer
Dan Buckley: President, Marvel Entertainment
Alan Fine: Executive Producer

IDW Publishing:

IDW

Chris Ryall, President and Publisher/CCO
John Barber, Editor-In-Chief
Robbie Robbins, EVP/Sr. Art Director
Cara Morrison, Chief Financial Officer
Matt Ruzicka, Chief Accounting Officer
Anita Frazier, SVP of Sales and Marketing
David Hedgecock, Associate Publisher
Jerry Bennington, VP of New Product Development
Lorelei Bunjes, VP of Digital Services
Justin Eisinger, Editorial Director, Graphic Novels & Collections
Eric Moss, Senior Director, Licensing and Business Development

Ted Adams, Founder of IDW

Collection Edits
JUSTIN EISINGER
and **ALONZO SIMON**

Collection Design
CHRISTA MIESNER

Cover Art by
JON SOMMARIVA

ISBN: 978-1-68405-515-9   22 21 20 19   1 2 3 4

Special thanks: **Tom Brevoort**, **Nick Lowe**, and **Sana Amanat**

MARVEL ACTION: AVENGERS: THE NEW DANGER (BOOK 1). APRIL 2019.
FIRST PRINTING. © 2019 MARVEL, LLC. The IDW logo is registered in the U.S. Patent
and Trademark Office. IDW Publishing, a division of Idea and Design Works, LLC. Editorial
offices: 2765 Truxtun Road, San Diego, CA 92106. Any similarities to persons living or dead are
purely coincidental. With the exception of artwork used for review purposes, none of
the contents of this publication may be reprinted without the permission of Idea and Design
Works, LLC.

Printed in Canada.

IDW Publishing does not read or accept unsolicited submissions
of ideas, stories, or artwork.

Originally published as MARVEL ACTION: AVENGERS issues #1–3.

For international rights, contact licensing@idwpublishing.com

MARVEL
MARVEL ACTION
AVENGERS
THE NEW DANGER

WRITTEN BY **MATTHEW K. MANNING**

ART BY **JON SOMMARIVA**

COLORS BY **PROTOBUNKER**

LETTERS BY **CHRISTA MIESNER**

ASSISTANT EDITS BY **MEGAN BROWN**

EDITED BY **BOBBY CURNOW**

EDITOR IN CHIEF **JOHN BARBER**

PUBLISHER **CHRIS RYALL**

AVENGERS CREATED BY **STAN LEE & JACK KIRBY**

ART BY: JON SOMMARIVA

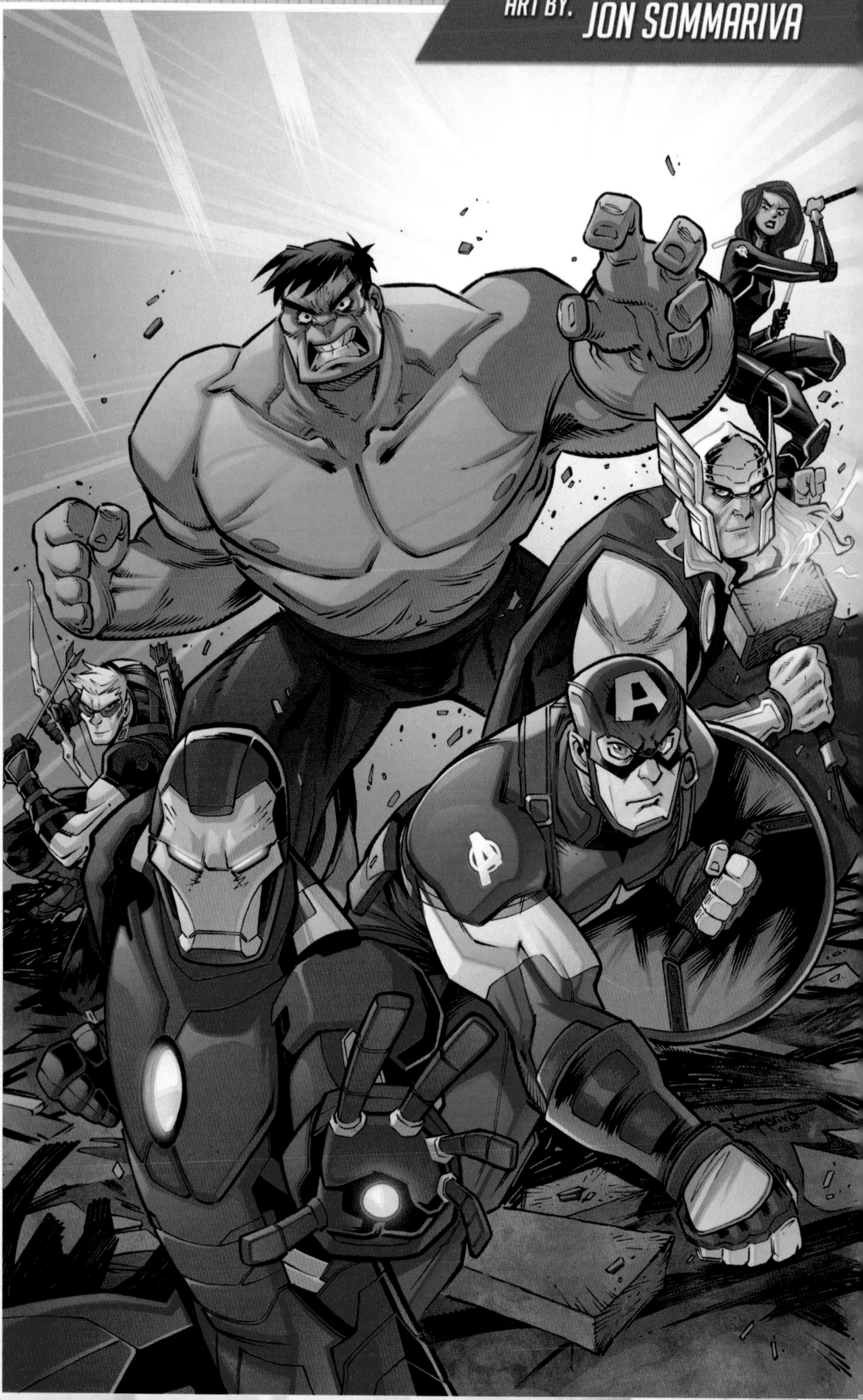

YOU ARE A.I.M.

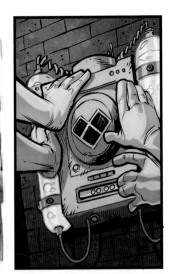

I AM A.I.M.

JUST GET THE SUIT AND GET OUT.

THE BRAINWAVE CONTROLS WILL BE WONKY AT FIRST, BUT I'M TRAINED FOR THIS.

I CAN DO IT.

PLEASE DON'T MESS THIS UP.

BOMB IS IN PLACE.

BEGIN COUNTDOWN...

...NOW.

BEEP

00:30

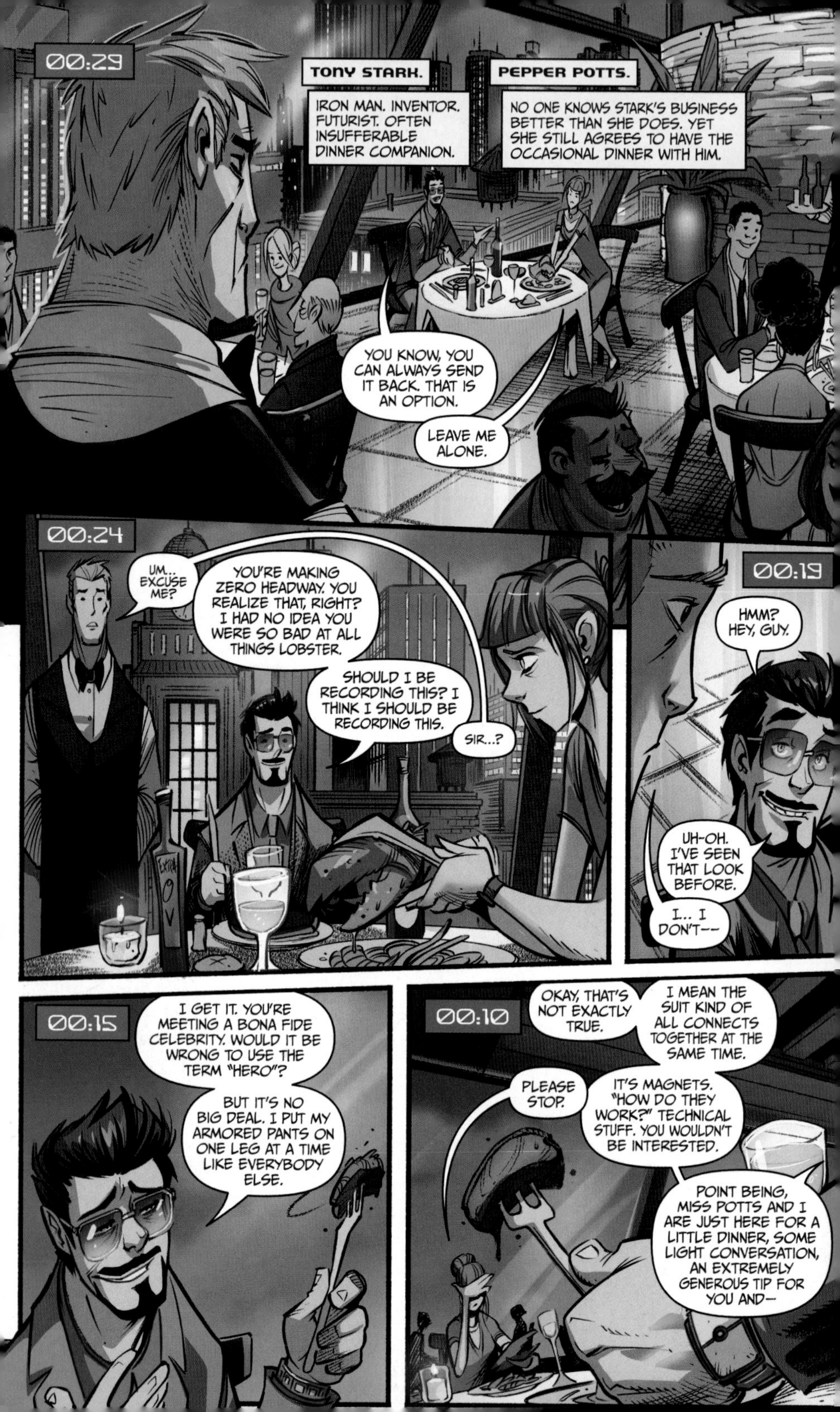
00:29
TONY STARK.
IRON MAN. INVENTOR. FUTURIST. OFTEN INSUFFERABLE DINNER COMPANION.
PEPPER POTTS.
NO ONE KNOWS STARK'S BUSINESS BETTER THAN SHE DOES. YET SHE STILL AGREES TO HAVE THE OCCASIONAL DINNER WITH HIM.
YOU KNOW, YOU CAN ALWAYS SEND IT BACK. THAT IS AN OPTION.
LEAVE ME ALONE.
00:24
UM... EXCUSE ME?
YOU'RE MAKING ZERO HEADWAY. YOU REALIZE THAT, RIGHT? I HAD NO IDEA YOU WERE SO BAD AT ALL THINGS LOBSTER.
SHOULD I BE RECORDING THIS? I THINK I SHOULD BE RECORDING THIS.
SIR...?
00:19
HMM? HEY, GUY.
UH-OH. I'VE SEEN THAT LOOK BEFORE.
I... I DON'T--
00:15
I GET IT. YOU'RE MEETING A BONA FIDE CELEBRITY. WOULD IT BE WRONG TO USE THE TERM "HERO"?
BUT IT'S NO BIG DEAL. I PUT MY ARMORED PANTS ON ONE LEG AT A TIME LIKE EVERYBODY ELSE.
00:10
OKAY, THAT'S NOT EXACTLY TRUE.
I MEAN THE SUIT KIND OF ALL CONNECTS TOGETHER AT THE SAME TIME.
PLEASE STOP.
IT'S MAGNETS. "HOW DO THEY WORK?" TECHNICAL STUFF. YOU WOULDN'T BE INTERESTED.
POINT BEING, MISS POTTS AND I ARE JUST HERE FOR A LITTLE DINNER, SOME LIGHT CONVERSATION, AN EXTREMELY GENEROUS TIP FOR YOU AND—

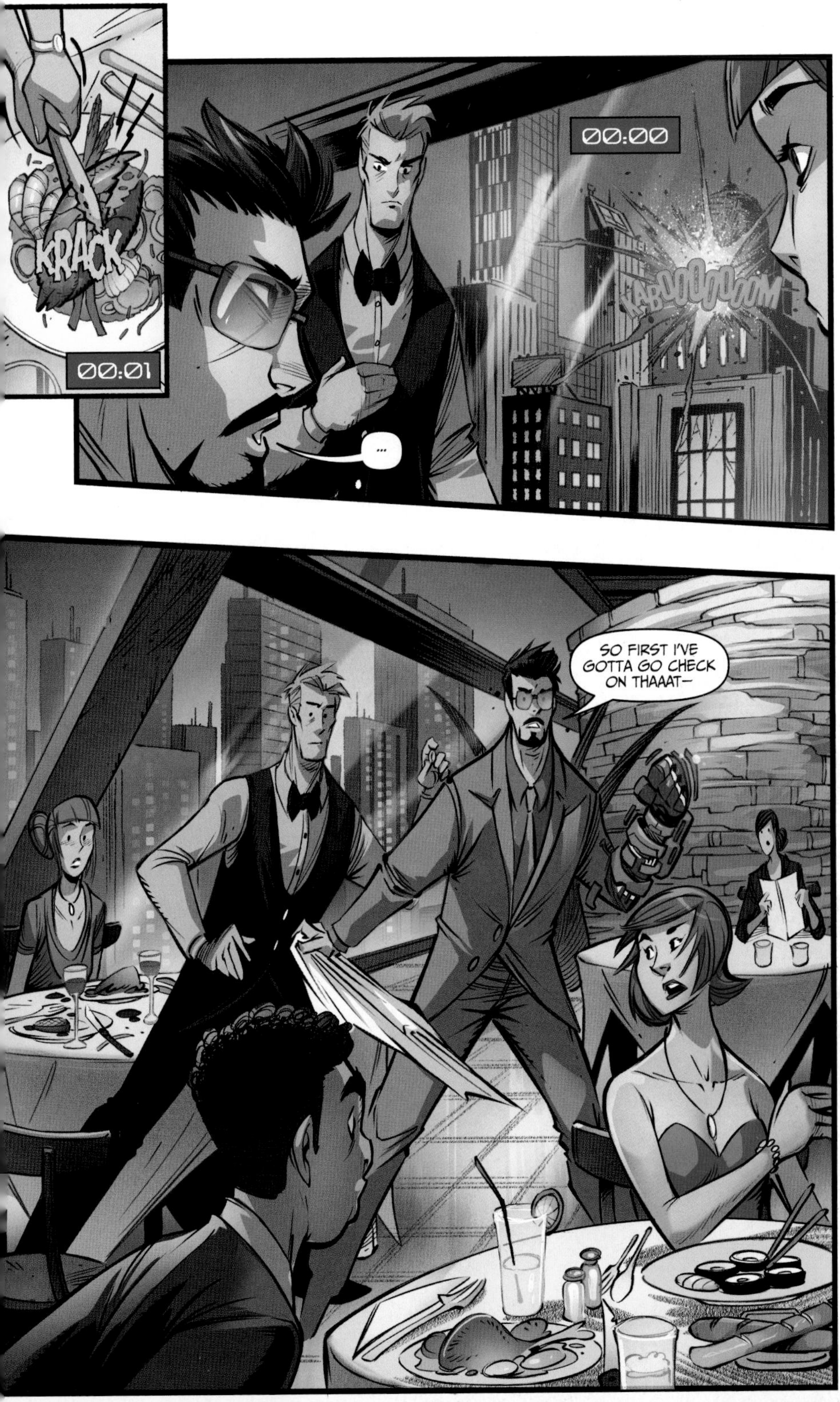
KRACK
00:01
00:00
KABOOOOOOM
...
SO FIRST I'VE GOTTA GO CHECK ON THAAAT—

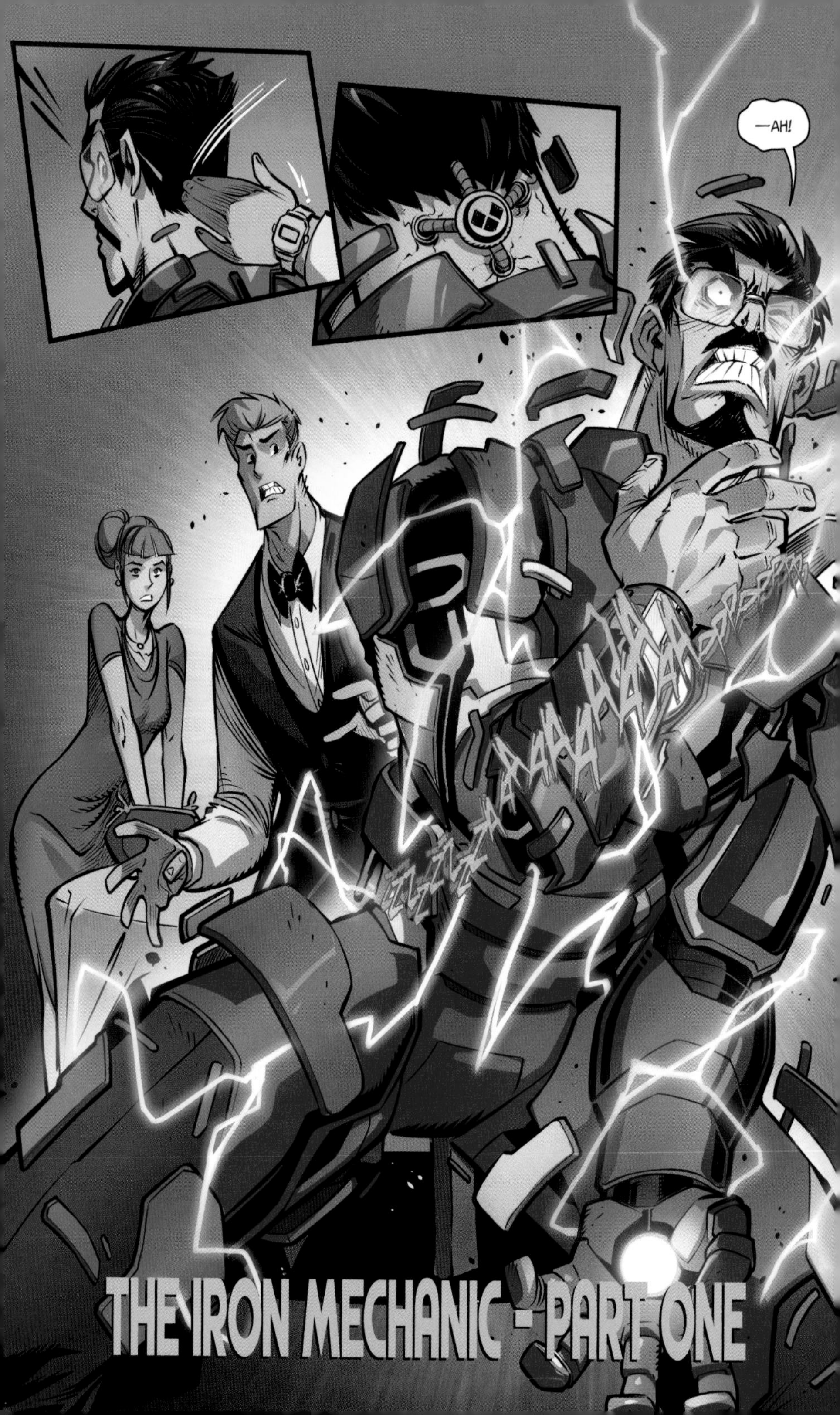
—AH!
THE IRON MECHANIC - PART ONE

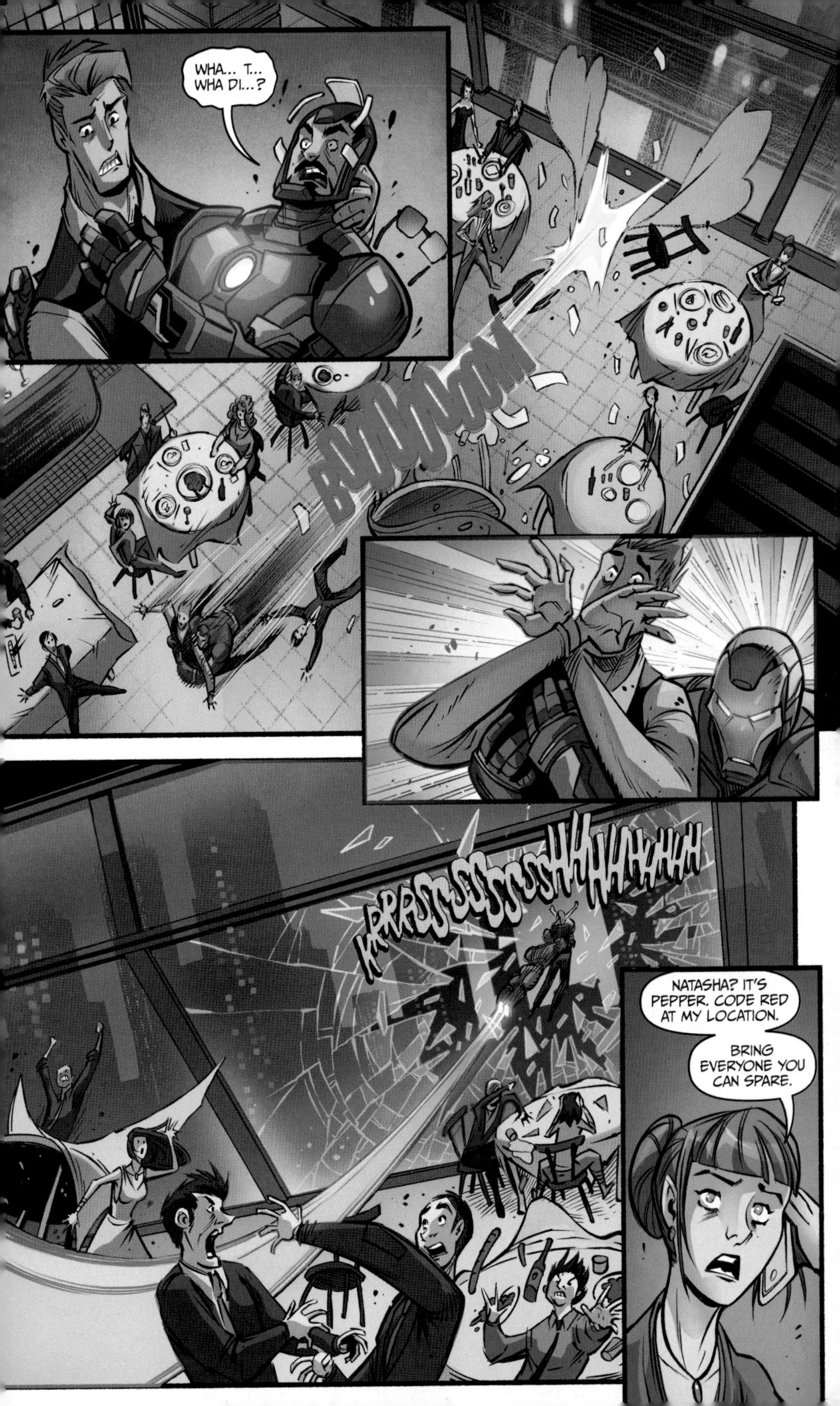
WHA... T...
WHA DI...?
BOOOOOOOM
KRRASSSSSSSSHHHHHHHHH
NATASHA? IT'S PEPPER. CODE RED AT MY LOCATION.
BRING EVERYONE YOU CAN SPARE.

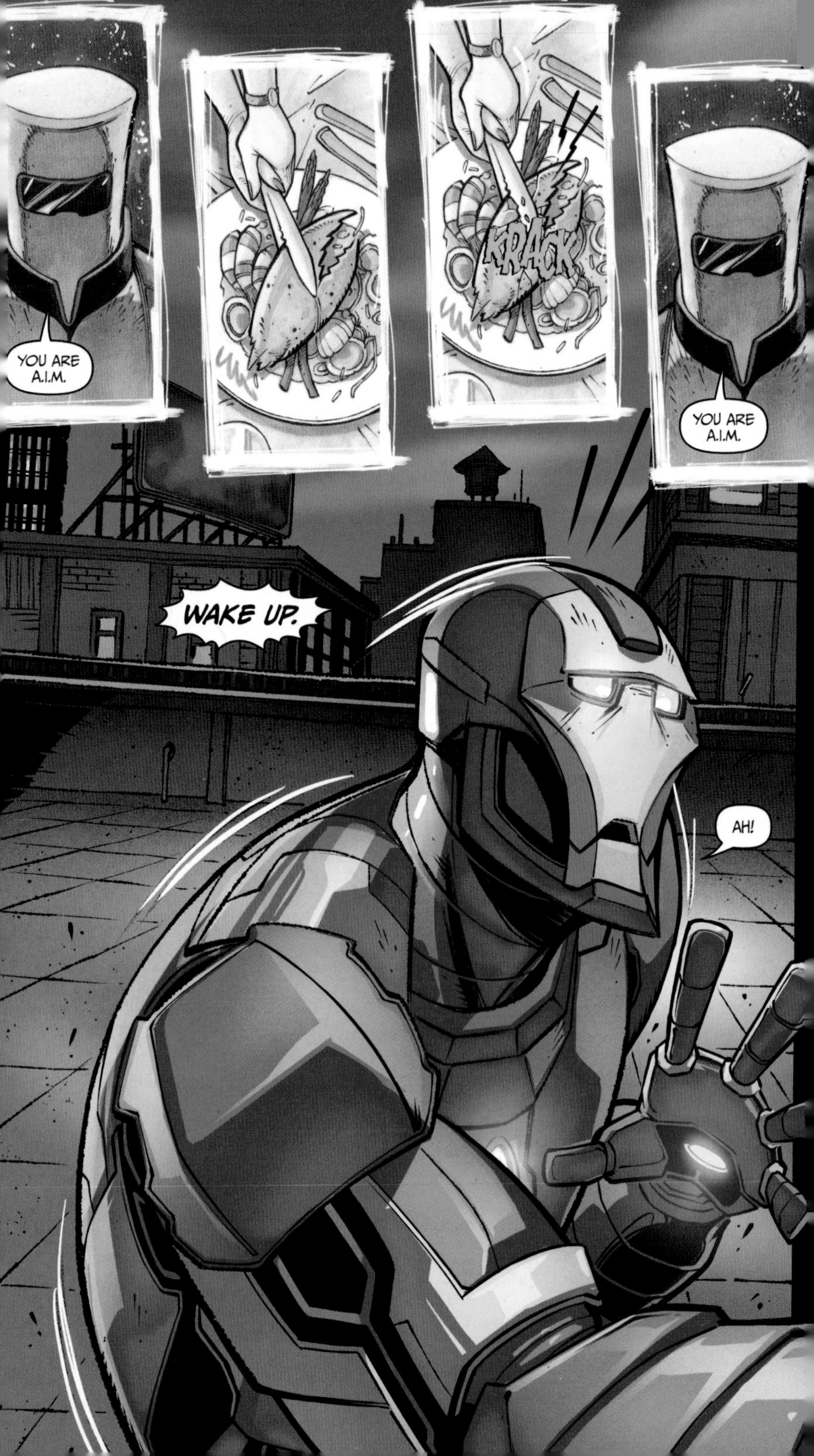
YOU ARE A.I.M.
KRACK
YOU ARE A.I.M.
WAKE UP.
AH!

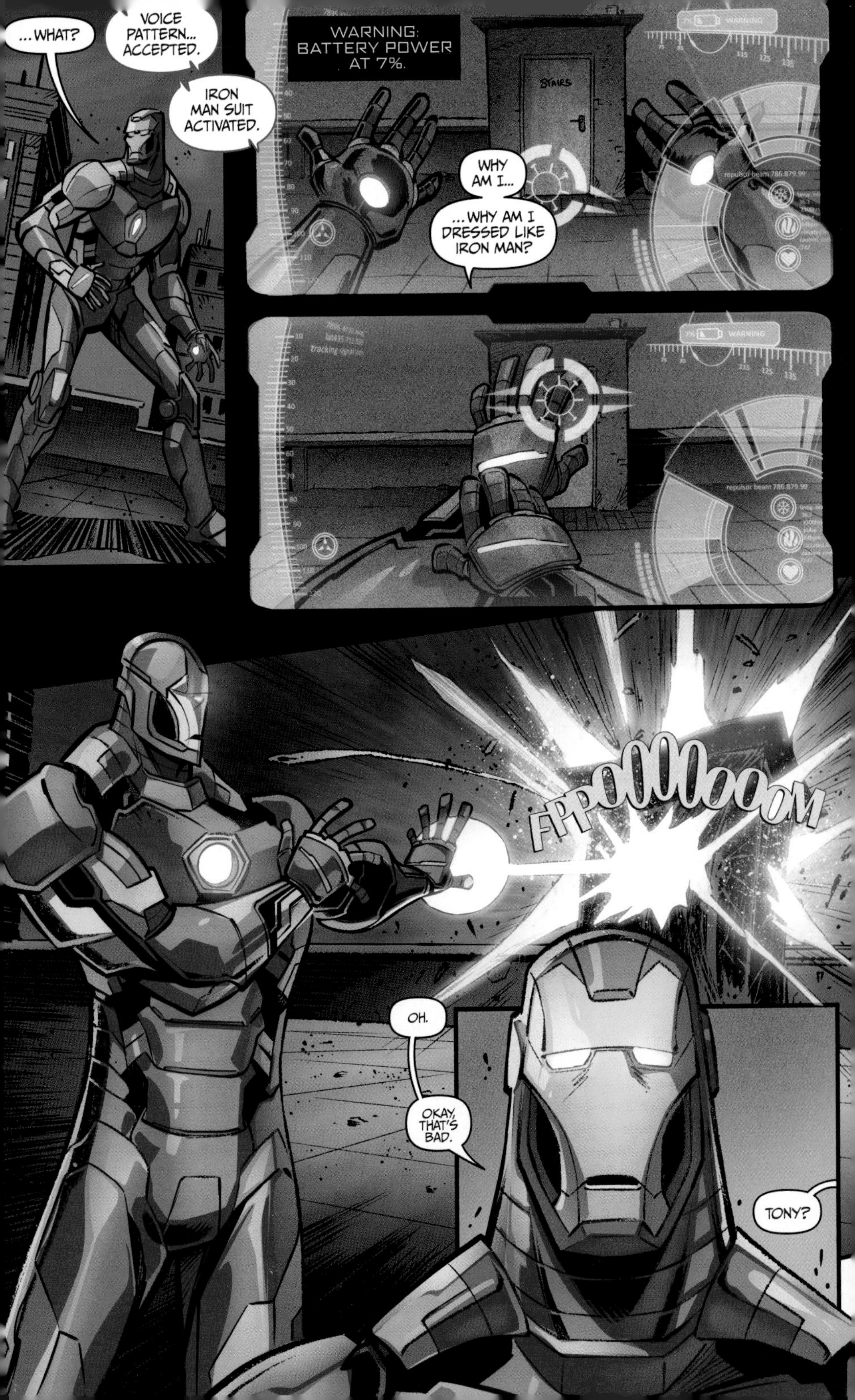
...WHAT?
VOICE PATTERN... ACCEPTED.
IRON MAN SUIT ACTIVATED.
WARNING: BATTERY POWER AT 7%.
STAIRS
WHY AM I...
...WHY AM I DRESSED LIKE IRON MAN?
7% WARNING
FPPOOOOOOOOM
OH.
OKAY, THAT'S BAD.
TONY?

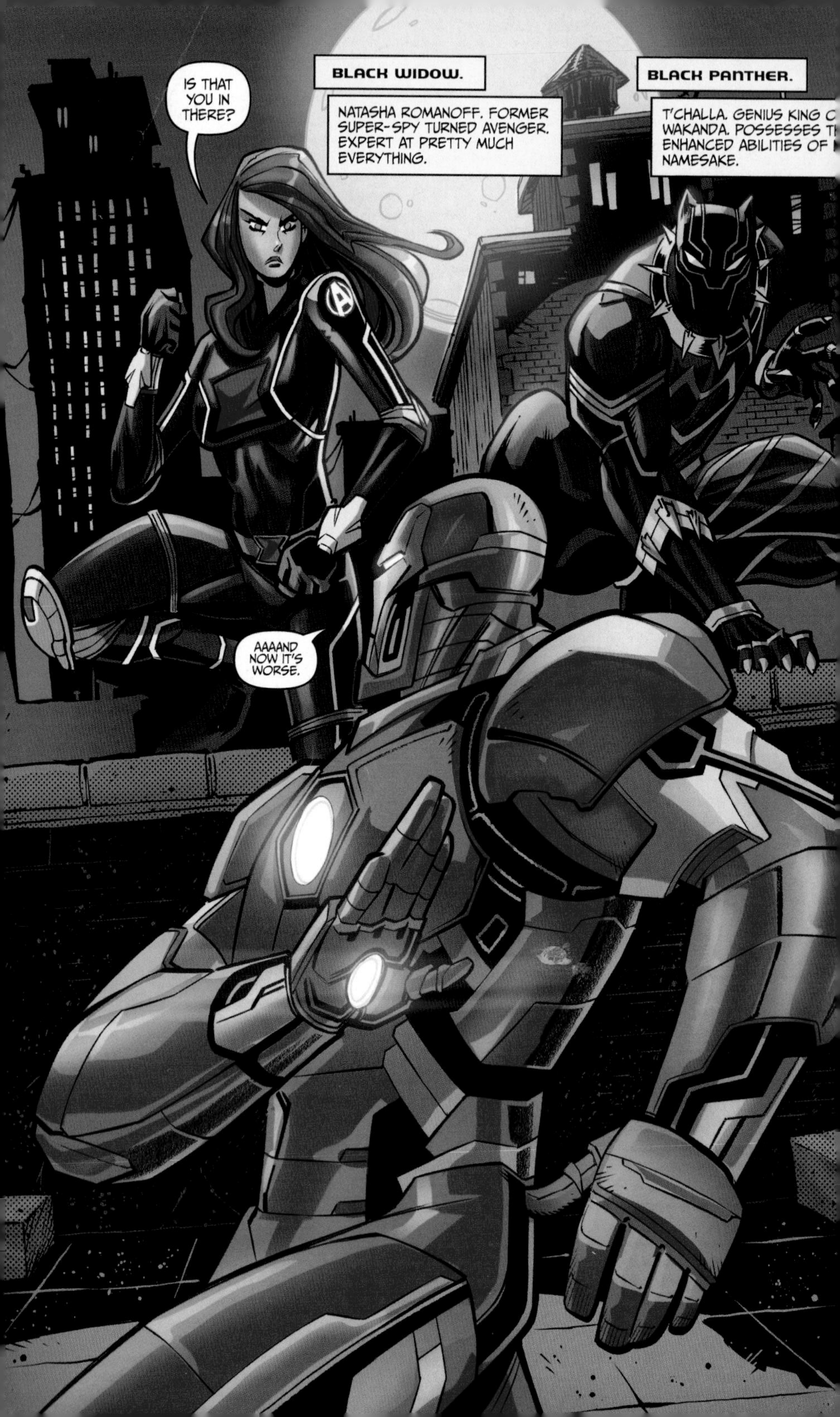
IS THAT YOU IN THERE?
BLACK WIDOW.
NATASHA ROMANOFF. FORMER SUPER-SPY TURNED AVENGER. EXPERT AT PRETTY MUCH EVERYTHING.
BLACK PANTHER.
T'CHALLA. GENIUS KING O WAKANDA. POSSESSES TH ENHANCED ABILITIES OF NAMESAKE.
AAAAND NOW IT'S WORSE.

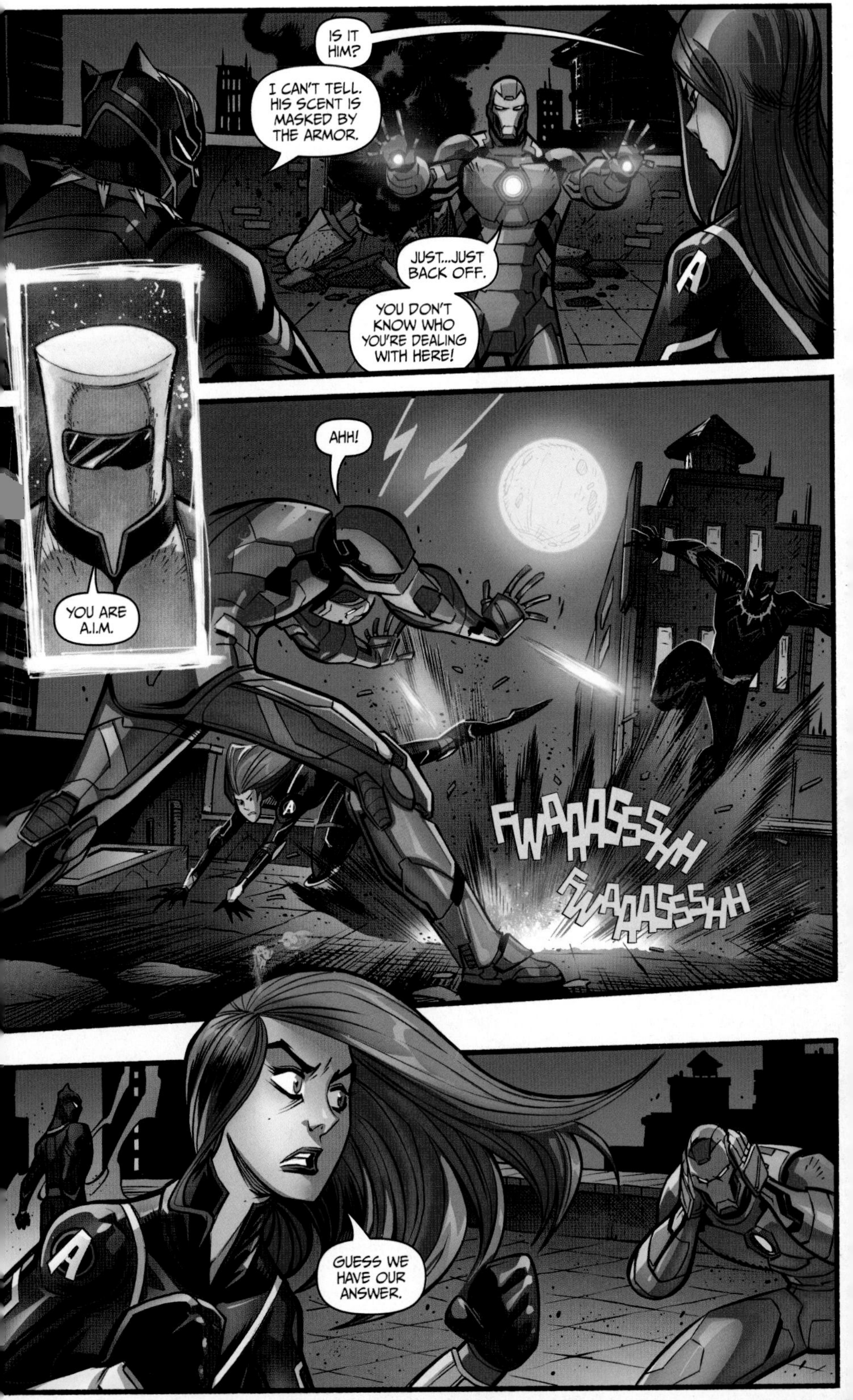
IS IT HIM?
I CAN'T TELL. HIS SCENT IS MASKED BY THE ARMOR.
JUST...JUST BACK OFF.
YOU DON'T KNOW WHO YOU'RE DEALING WITH HERE!
YOU ARE A.I.M.
AHH!
FWAAASSSHH
FWAAASSSHH
GUESS WE HAVE OUR ANSWER.

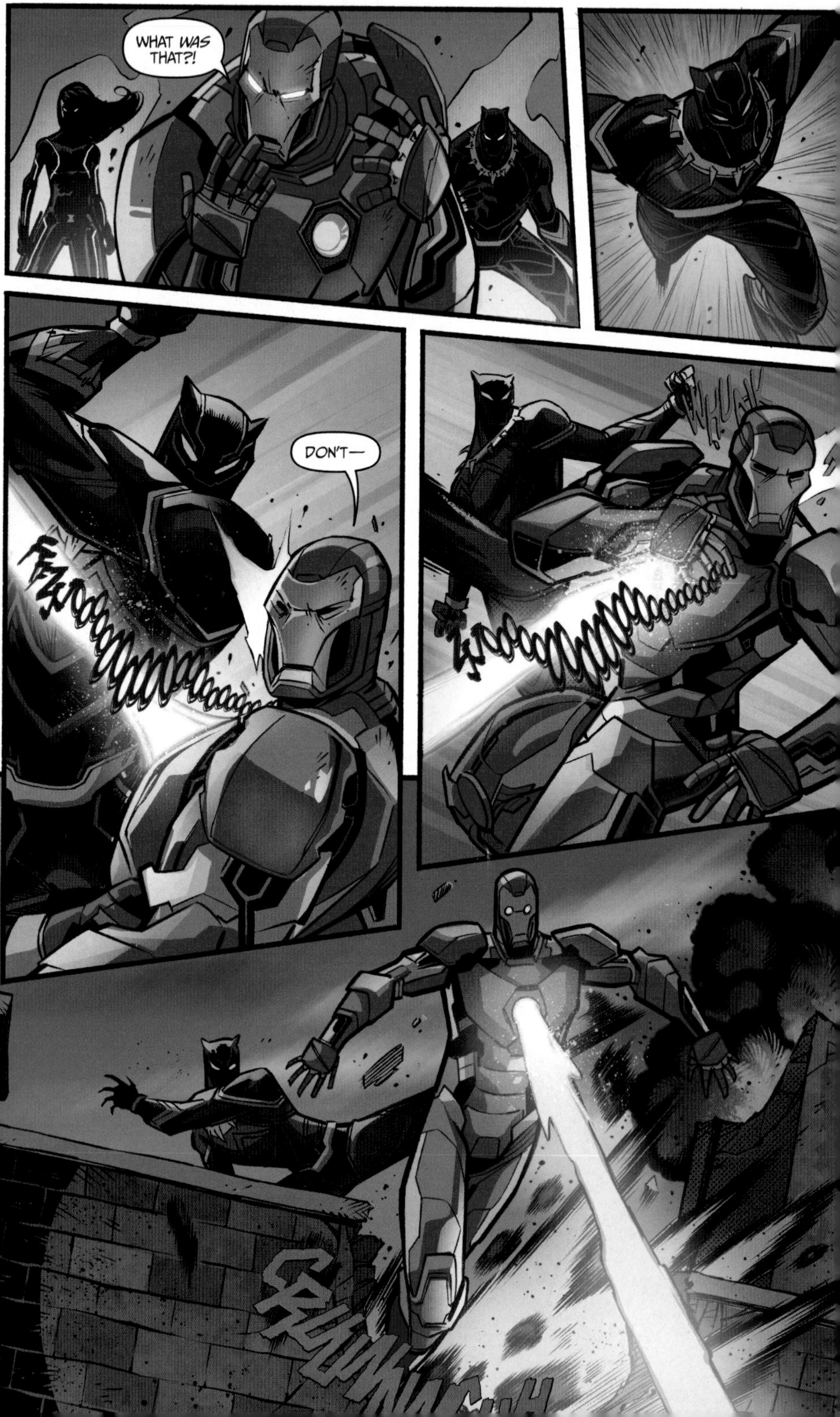
WHAT WAS THAT?!
DON'T—

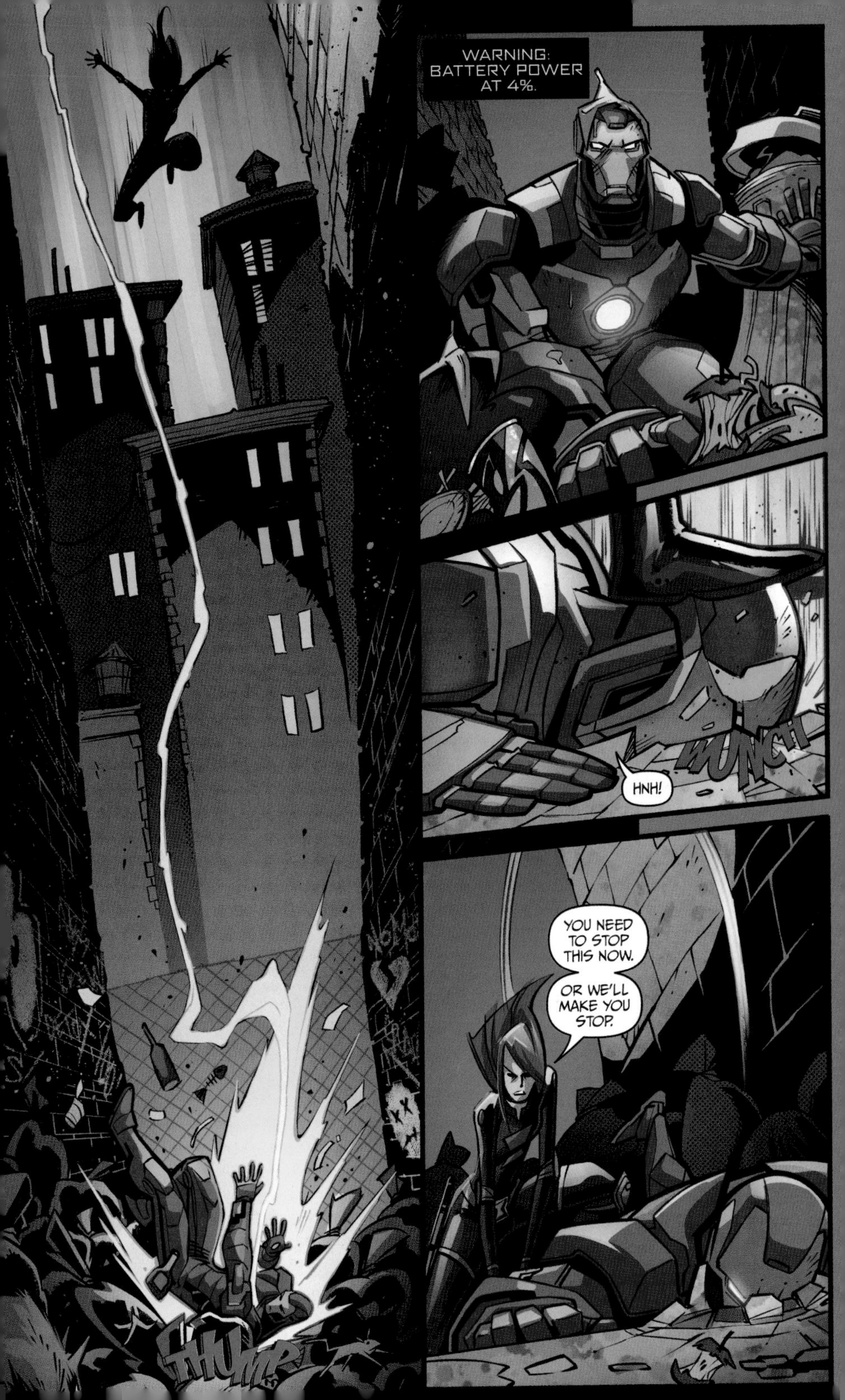
THUMP
WARNING: BATTERY POWER AT 4%.
HNH!
WUNCH
YOU NEED TO STOP THIS NOW.
OR WE'LL MAKE YOU STOP.

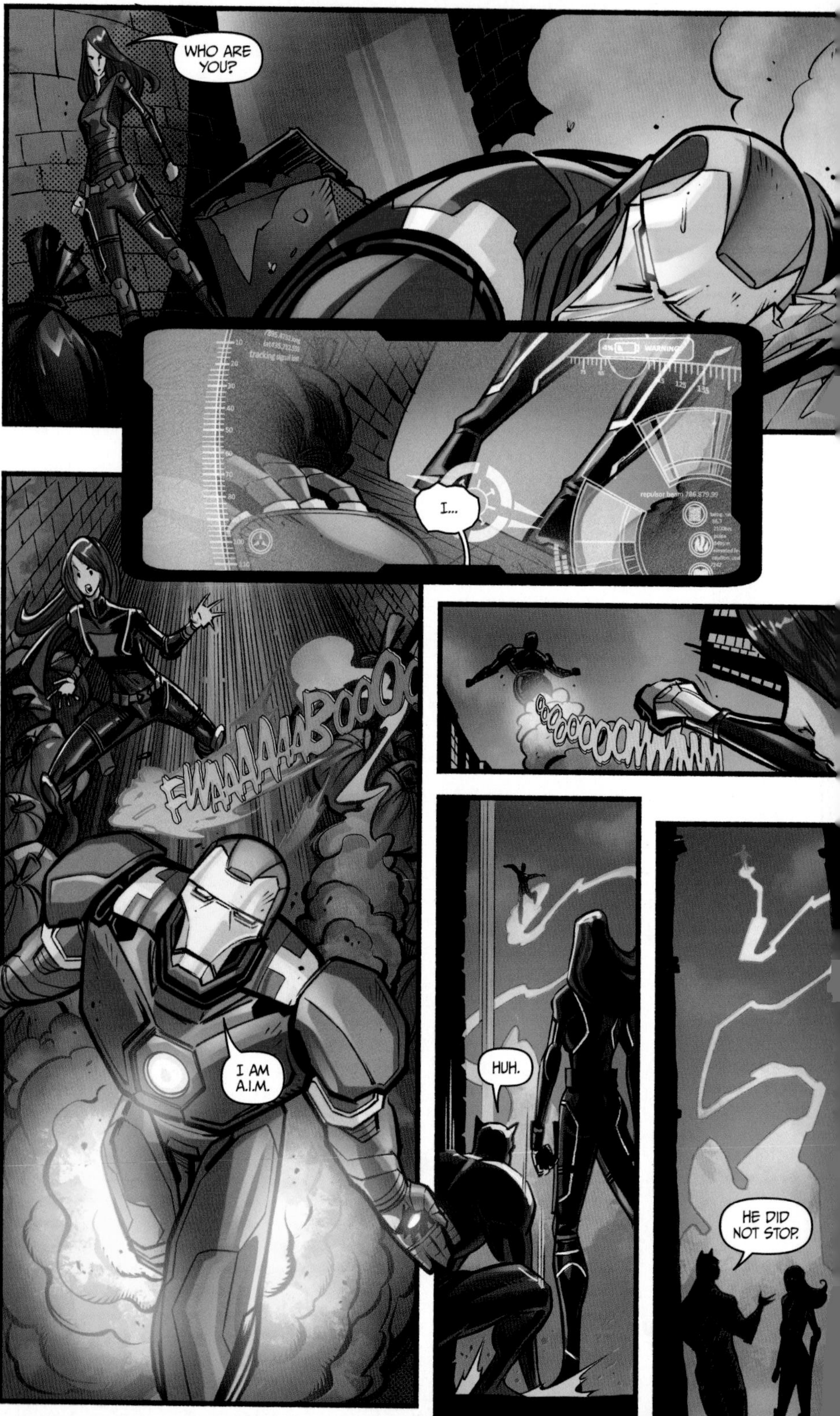
WHO ARE YOU?
WARNING
I...
I AM A.I.M.
HUH.
HE DID NOT STOP.

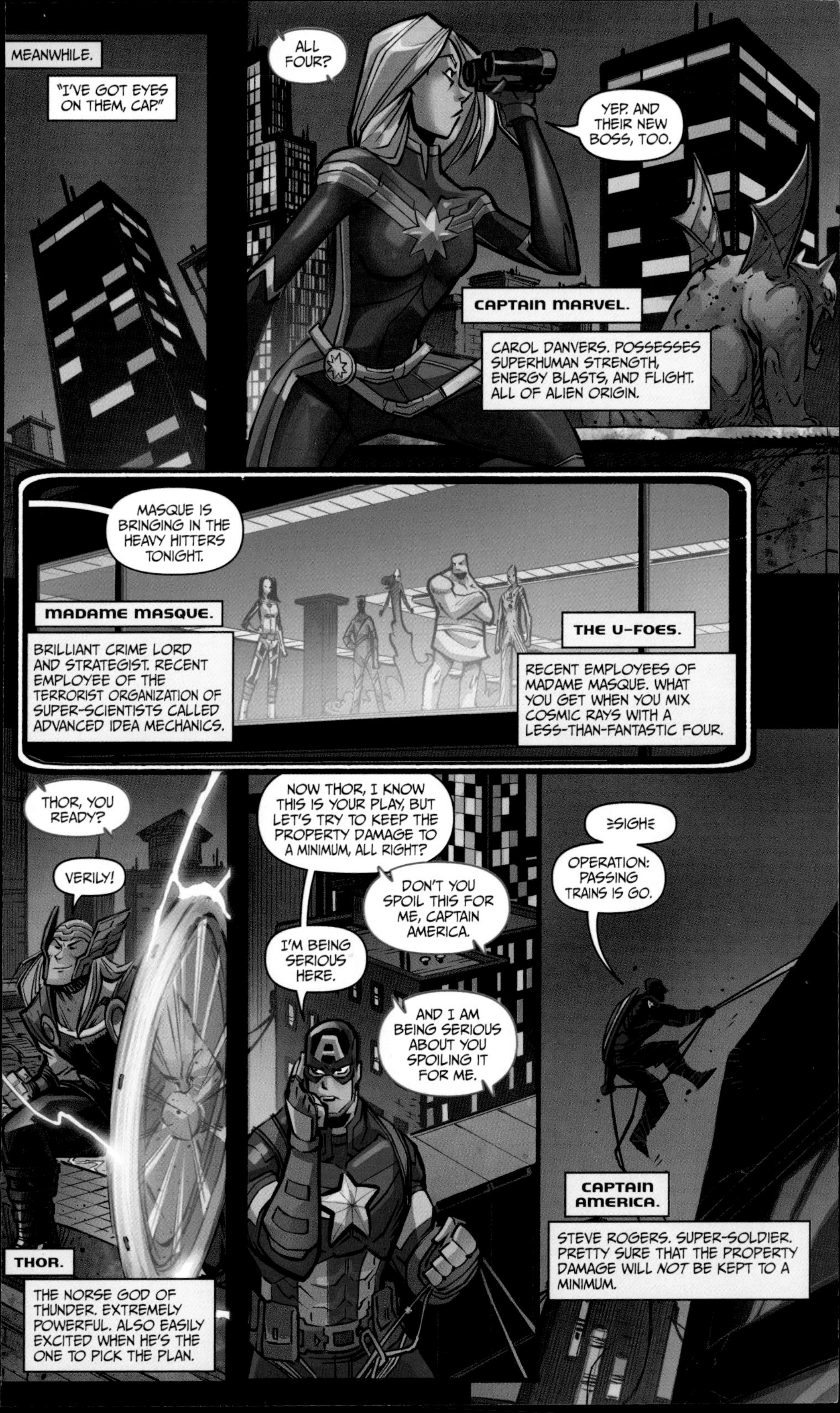
MEANWHILE.
"I'VE GOT EYES ON THEM, CAP."
ALL FOUR?
YEP. AND THEIR NEW BOSS, TOO.
CAPTAIN MARVEL.
CAROL DANVERS. POSSESSES SUPERHUMAN STRENGTH, ENERGY BLASTS, AND FLIGHT. ALL OF ALIEN ORIGIN.
MASQUE IS BRINGING IN THE HEAVY HITTERS TONIGHT.
MADAME MASQUE.
BRILLIANT CRIME LORD AND STRATEGIST. RECENT EMPLOYEE OF THE TERRORIST ORGANIZATION OF SUPER-SCIENTISTS CALLED ADVANCED IDEA MECHANICS.
THE U-FOES.
RECENT EMPLOYEES OF MADAME MASQUE. WHAT YOU GET WHEN YOU MIX COSMIC RAYS WITH A LESS-THAN-FANTASTIC FOUR.
THOR, YOU READY?
VERILY!
THOR.
THE NORSE GOD OF THUNDER. EXTREMELY POWERFUL. ALSO EASILY EXCITED WHEN HE'S THE ONE TO PICK THE PLAN.
NOW THOR, I KNOW THIS IS YOUR PLAY, BUT LET'S TRY TO KEEP THE PROPERTY DAMAGE TO A MINIMUM, ALL RIGHT?
DON'T YOU SPOIL THIS FOR ME, CAPTAIN AMERICA.
I'M BEING SERIOUS HERE.
AND I AM BEING SERIOUS ABOUT YOU SPOILING IT FOR ME.
SIGH
OPERATION: PASSING TRAINS IS GO.
CAPTAIN AMERICA.
STEVE ROGERS. SUPER-SOLDIER. PRETTY SURE THAT THE PROPERTY DAMAGE WILL *NOT* BE KEPT TO A MINIMUM.

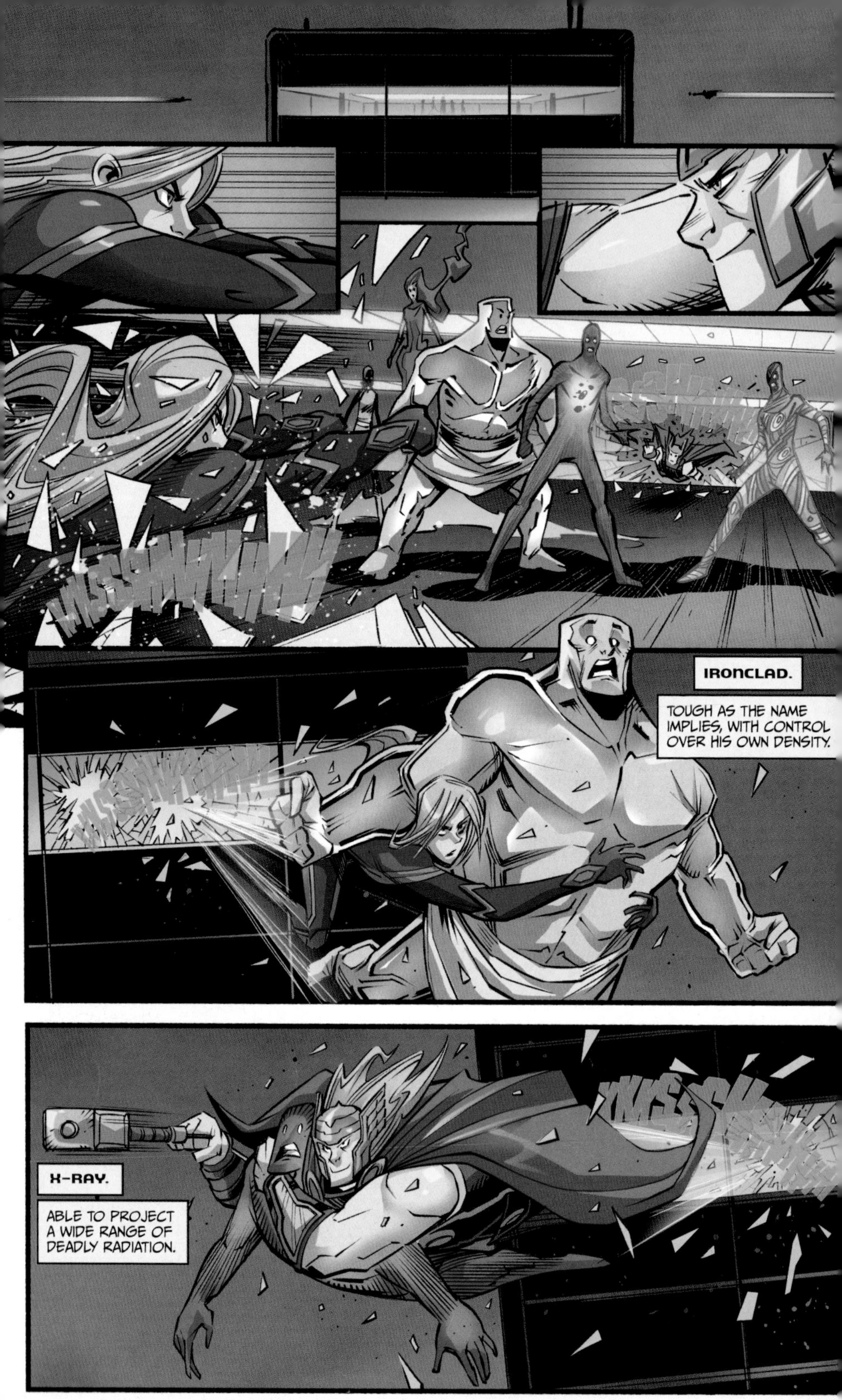

IRONCLAD.
TOUGH AS THE NAME IMPLIES, WITH CONTROL OVER HIS OWN DENSITY.
X-RAY.
ABLE TO PROJECT A WIDE RANGE OF DEADLY RADIATION.

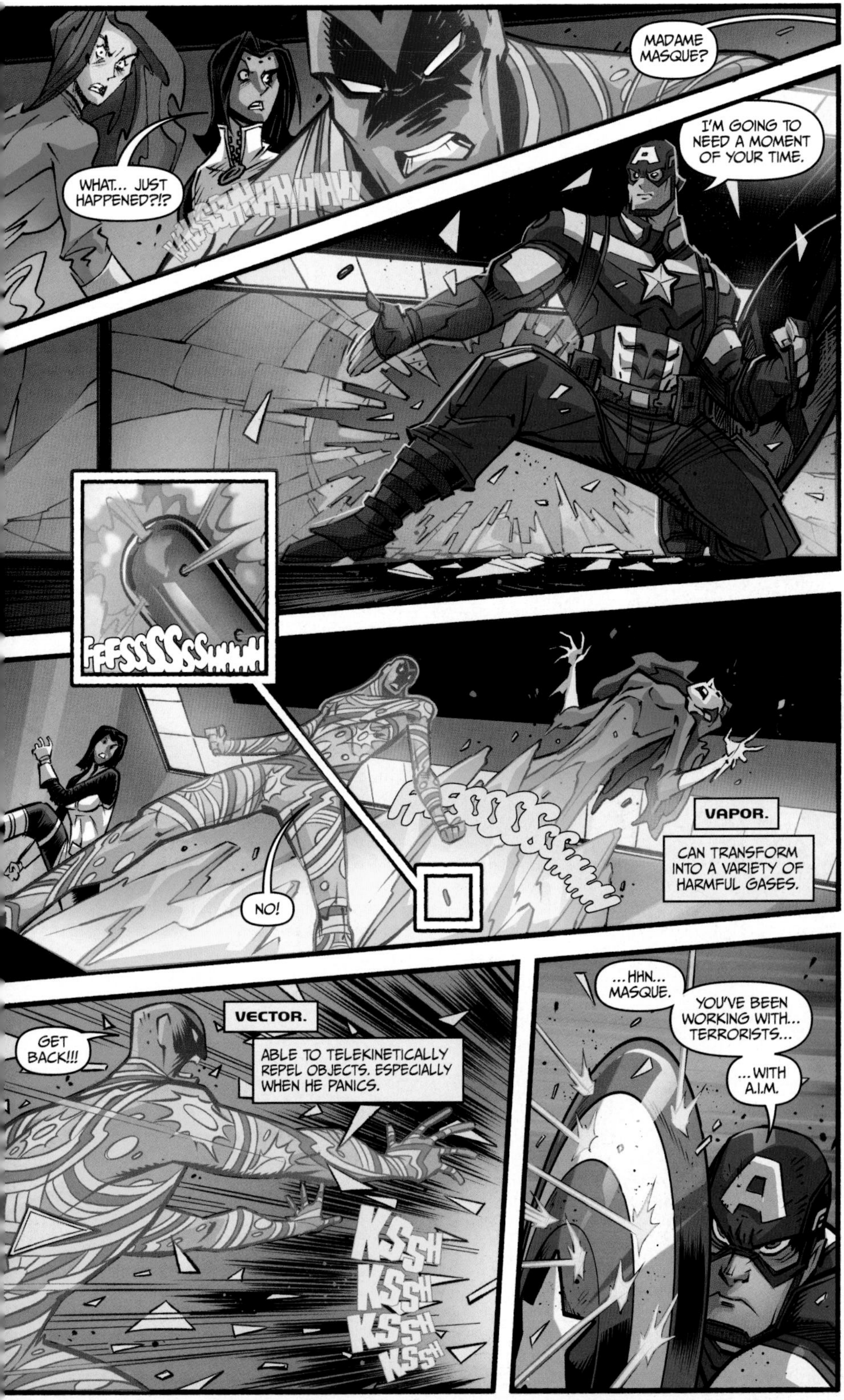

MADAME MASQUE?
WHAT... JUST HAPPENED?!?
I'M GOING TO NEED A MOMENT OF YOUR TIME.
FFFSSSSSSHHHHH
VAPOR.
CAN TRANSFORM INTO A VARIETY OF HARMFUL GASES.
NO!
VECTOR.
ABLE TO TELEKINETICALLY REPEL OBJECTS. ESPECIALLY WHEN HE PANICS.
GET BACK!!!
KSSH KSSH KSSH KSSH
...HHN... MASQUE.
YOU'VE BEEN WORKING WITH... TERRORISTS...
...WITH A.I.M.

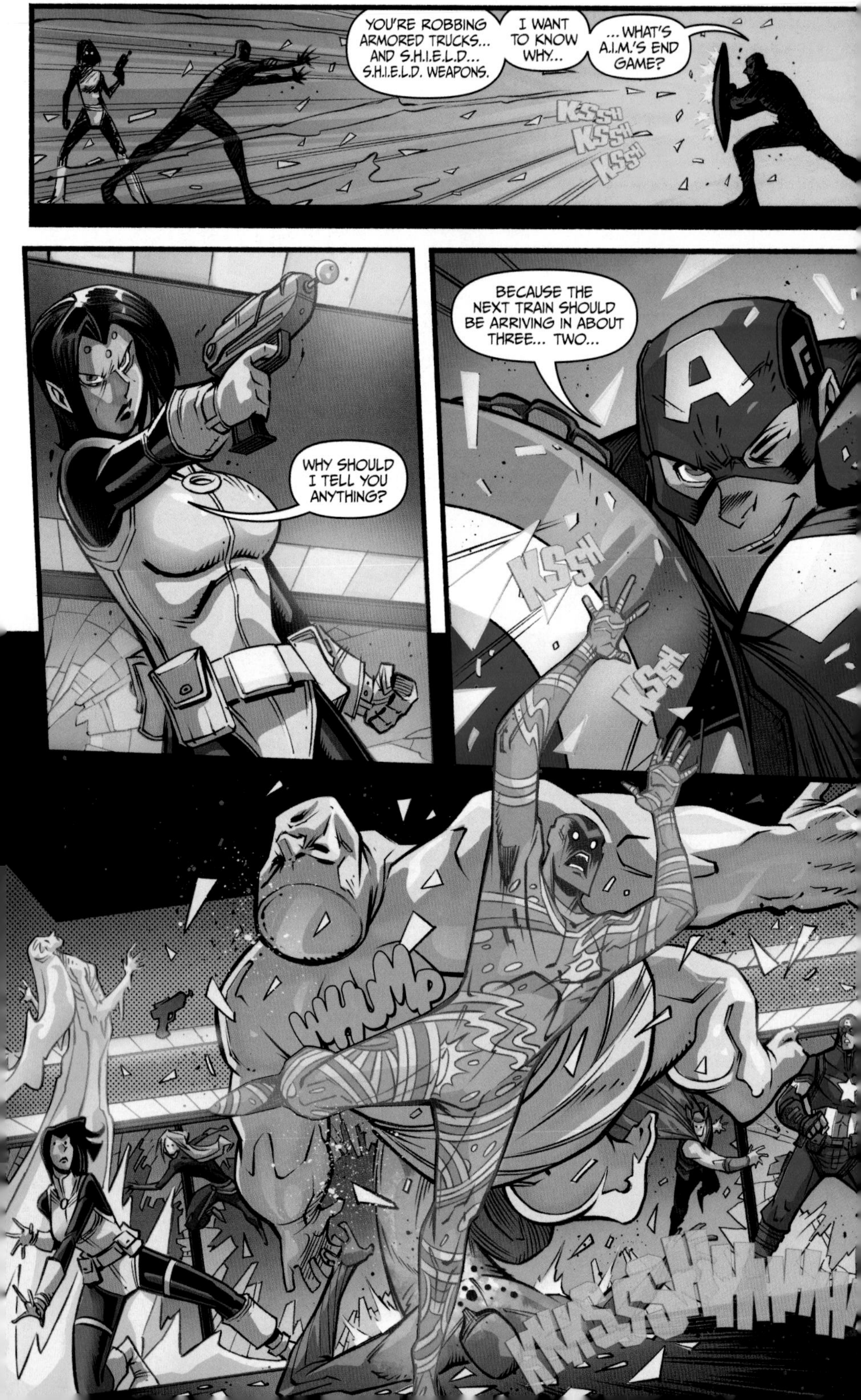

YOU'RE ROBBING ARMORED TRUCKS... AND S.H.I.E.L.D... S.H.I.E.L.D. WEAPONS.
I WANT TO KNOW WHY...
...WHAT'S A.I.M.'S END GAME?
KSSH
KSSH
KSSH
WHY SHOULD I TELL YOU ANYTHING?
BECAUSE THE NEXT TRAIN SHOULD BE ARRIVING IN ABOUT THREE... TWO...
KSSH
KSSH
WHUMP

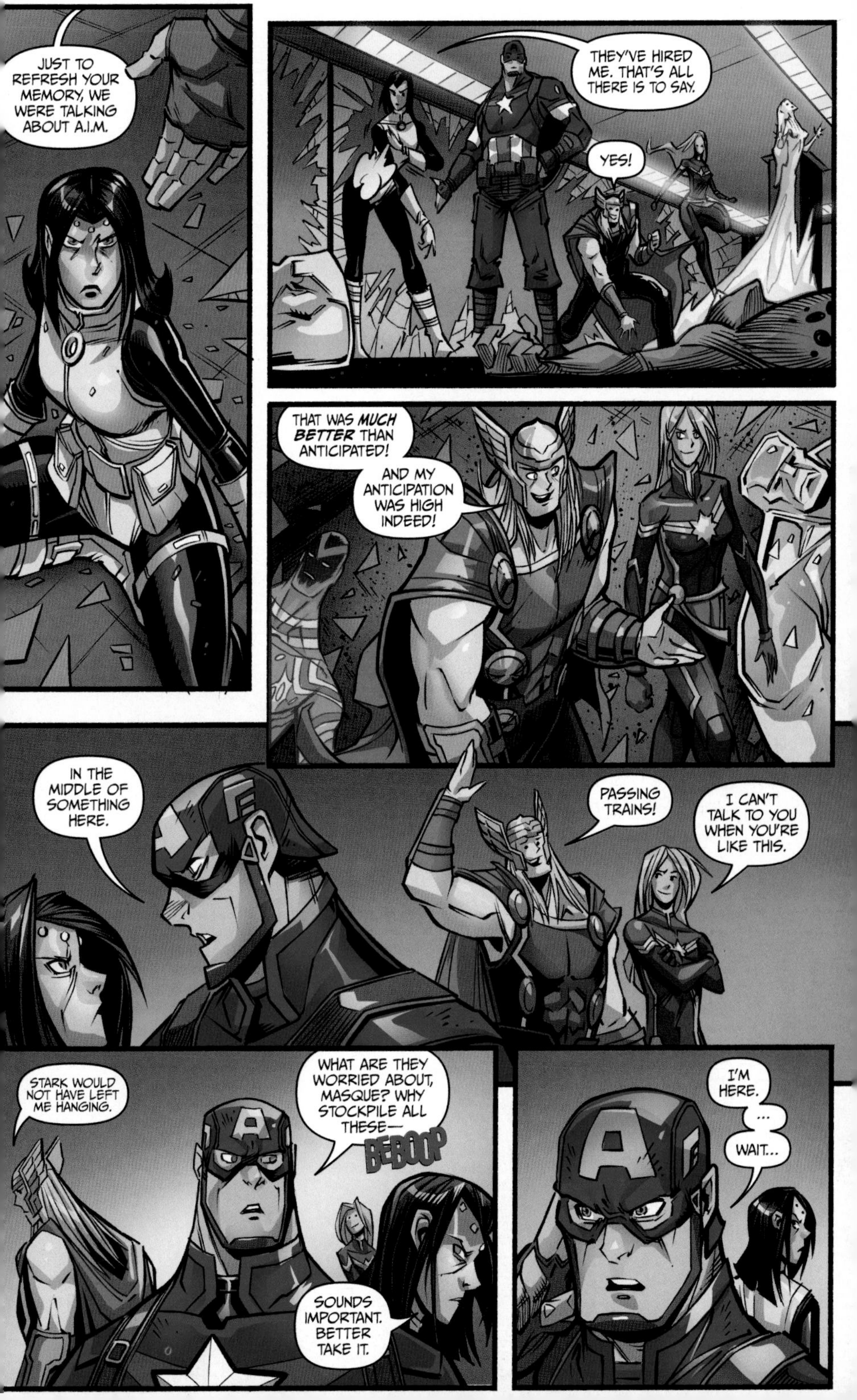
JUST TO REFRESH YOUR MEMORY, WE WERE TALKING ABOUT A.I.M.
THEY'VE HIRED ME. THAT'S ALL THERE IS TO SAY.
YES!
THAT WAS **MUCH BETTER** THAN ANTICIPATED!
AND MY ANTICIPATION WAS HIGH INDEED!
IN THE MIDDLE OF SOMETHING HERE.
PASSING TRAINS!
I CAN'T TALK TO YOU WHEN YOU'RE LIKE THIS.
STARK WOULD NOT HAVE LEFT ME HANGING.
WHAT ARE THEY WORRIED ABOUT, MASQUE? WHY STOCKPILE ALL THESE—
BEBOOP
SOUNDS IMPORTANT. BETTER TAKE IT.
I'M HERE.
...
WAIT...

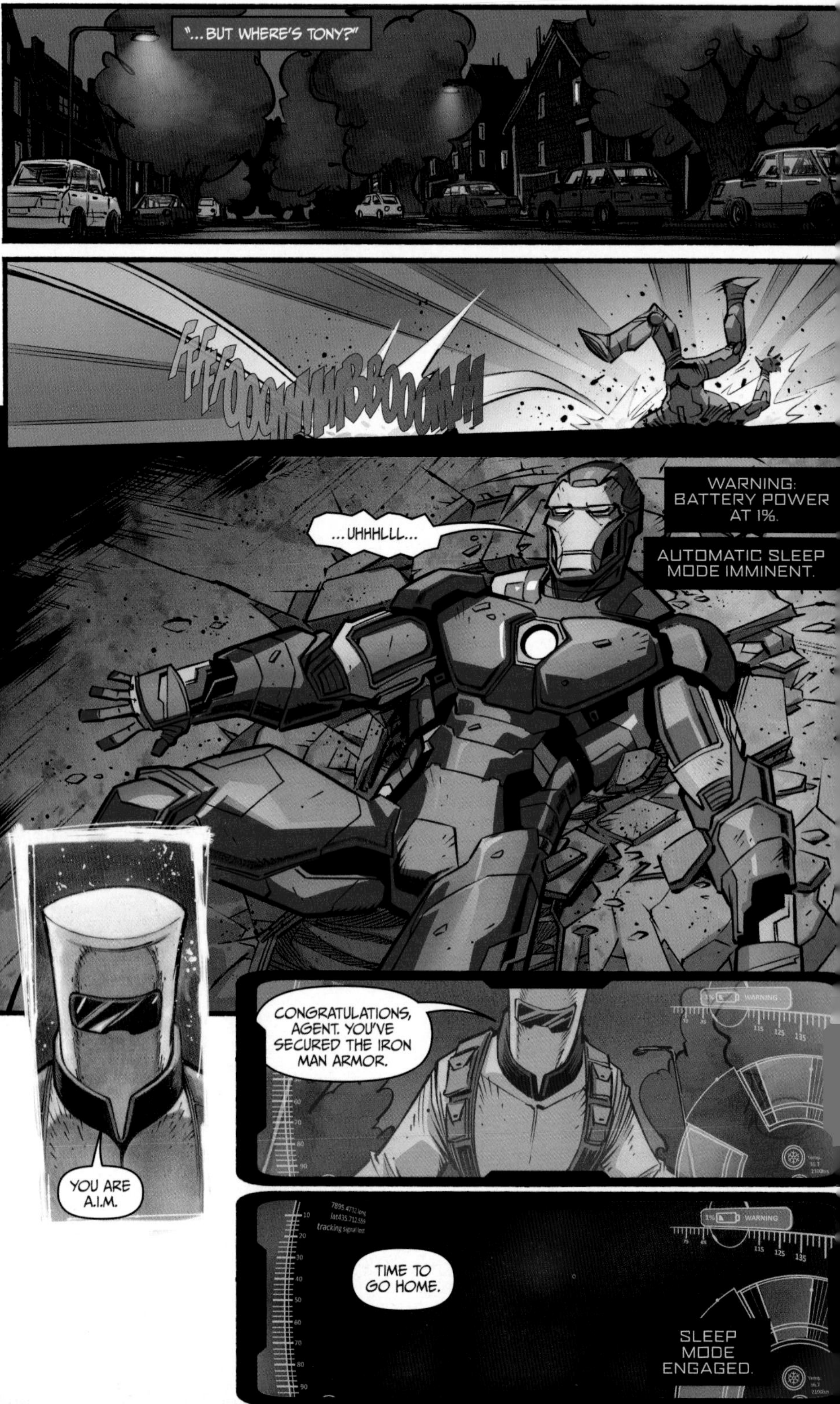
"...BUT WHERE'S TONY?"
FFFFOOOMMMBBOOOMM
WARNING: BATTERY POWER AT 1%.
AUTOMATIC SLEEP MODE IMMINENT.
...UHHHLLL...
YOU ARE A.I.M.
CONGRATULATIONS, AGENT. YOU'VE SECURED THE IRON MAN ARMOR.
WARNING
TIME TO GO HOME.
WARNING
SLEEP MODE ENGAGED.

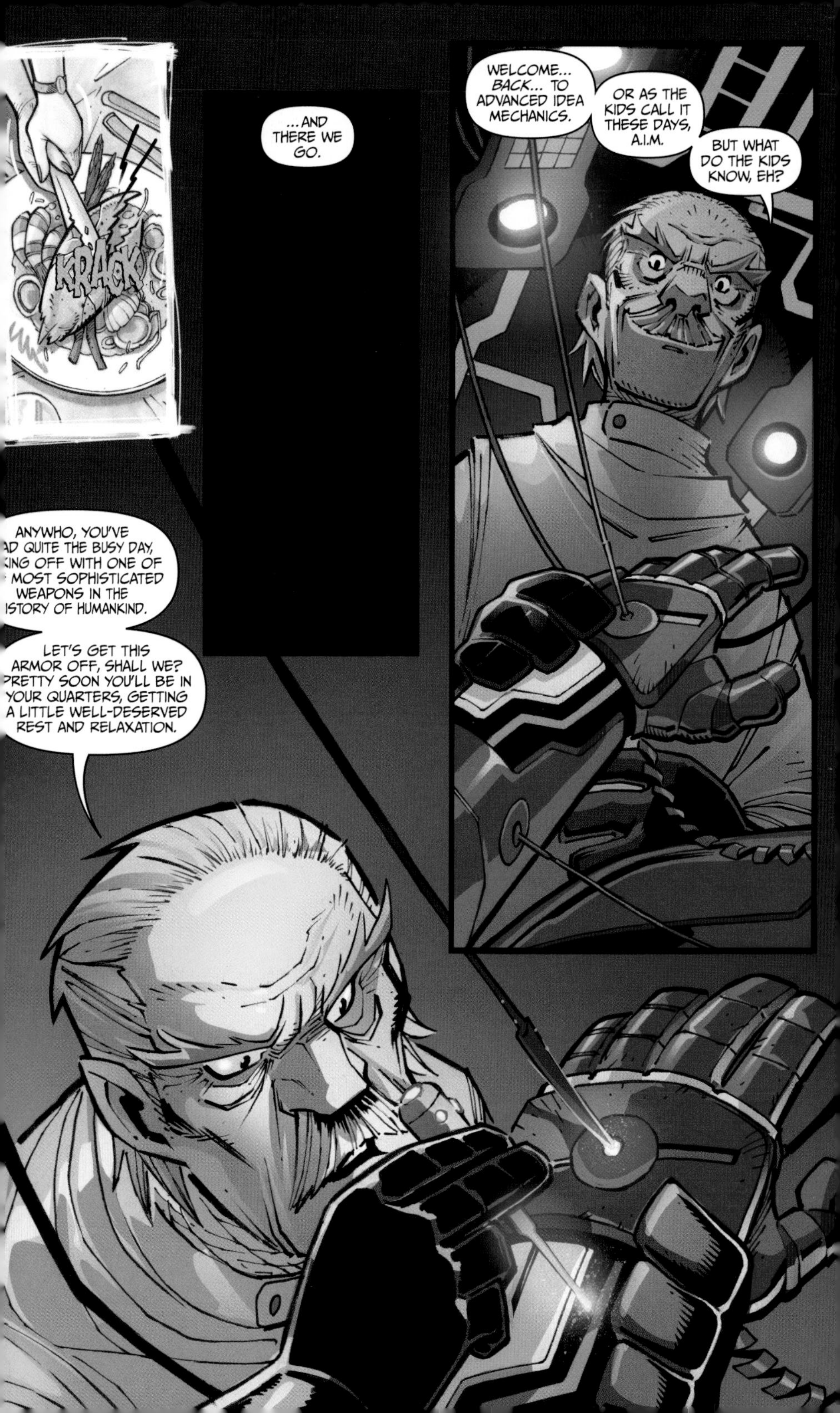
KRACK
...AND THERE WE GO.
WELCOME... BACK... TO ADVANCED IDEA MECHANICS.
OR AS THE KIDS CALL IT THESE DAYS, A.I.M.
BUT WHAT DO THE KIDS KNOW, EH?
ANYWHO, YOU'VE AD QUITE THE BUSY DAY, KING OFF WITH ONE OF MOST SOPHISTICATED WEAPONS IN THE ISTORY OF HUMANKIND.
LET'S GET THIS ARMOR OFF, SHALL WE? PRETTY SOON YOU'LL BE IN YOUR QUARTERS, GETTING A LITTLE WELL-DESERVED REST AND RELAXATION.

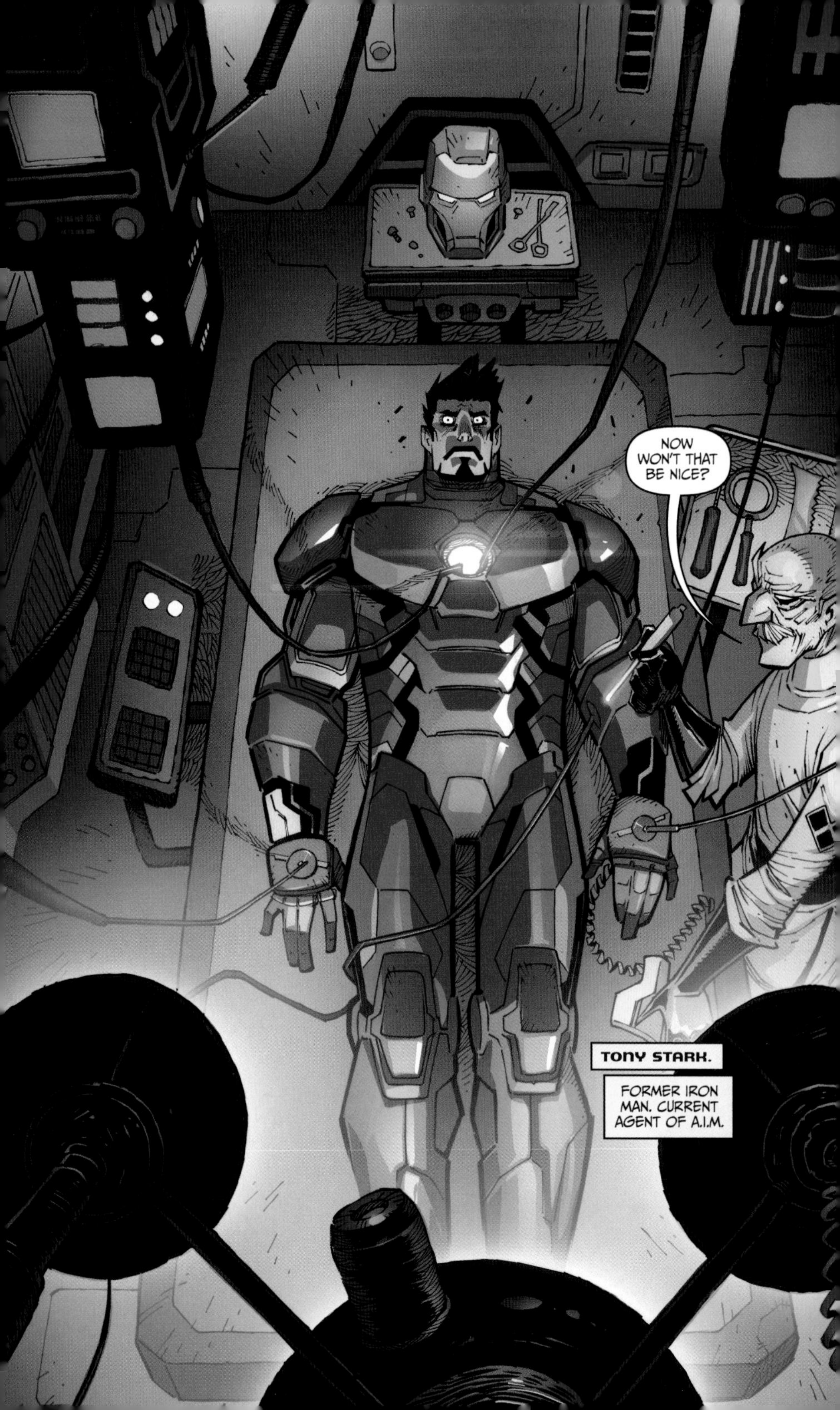

NOW WON'T THAT BE NICE?
TONY STARK.
FORMER IRON MAN. CURRENT AGENT OF A.I.M.

ART BY: SARA PITRE-DUROCHER

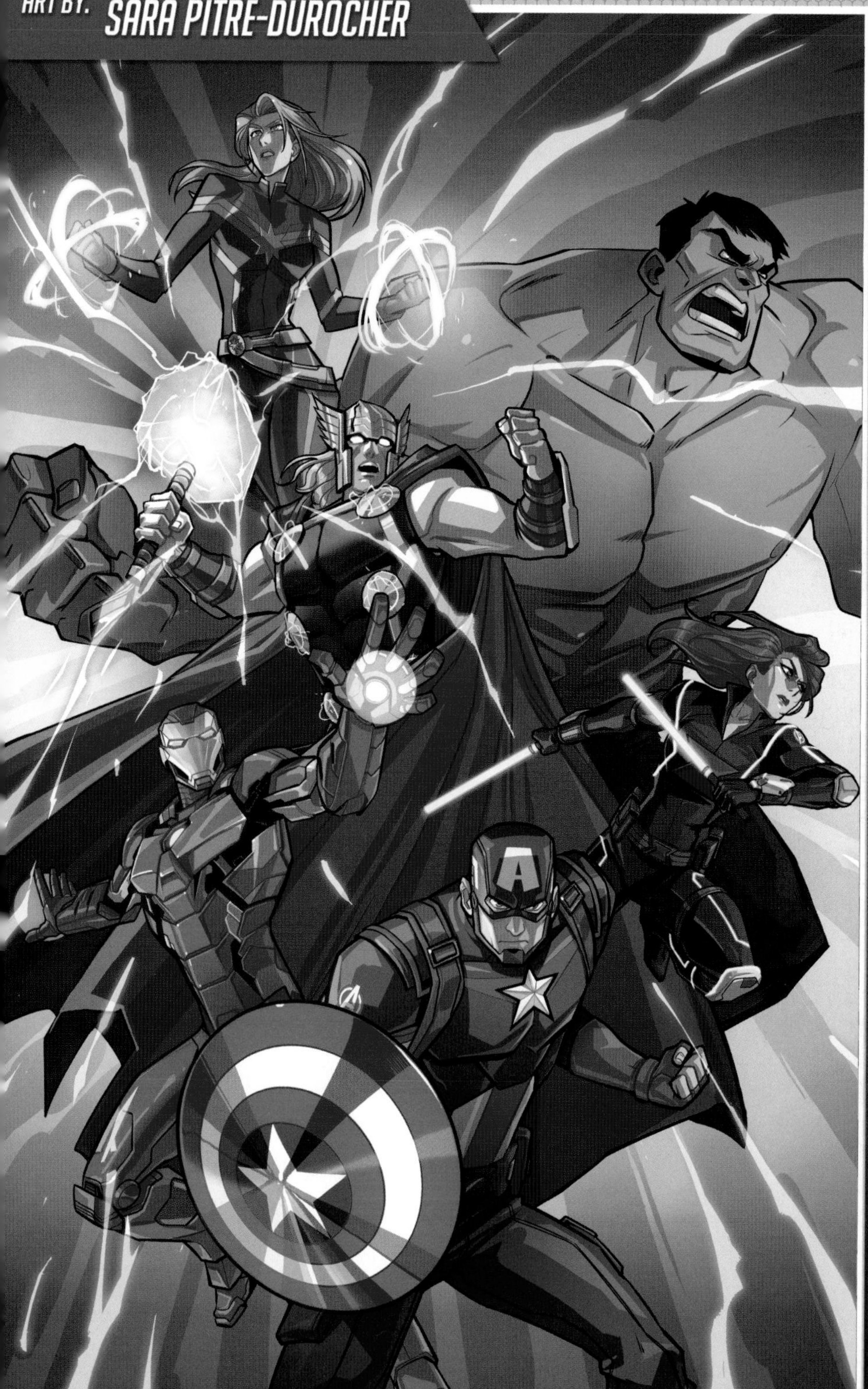

ART BY: JON SOMMARIVA

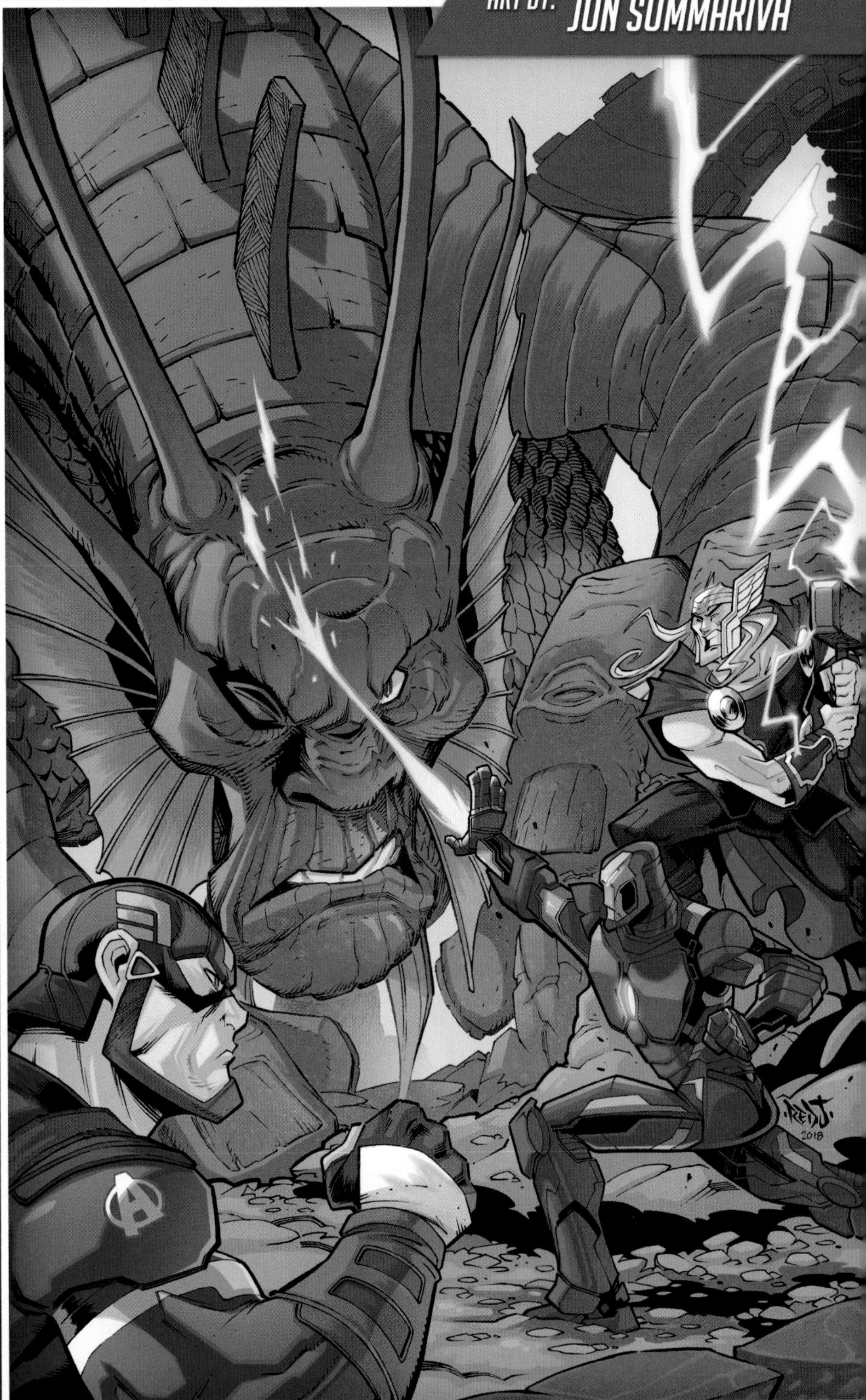

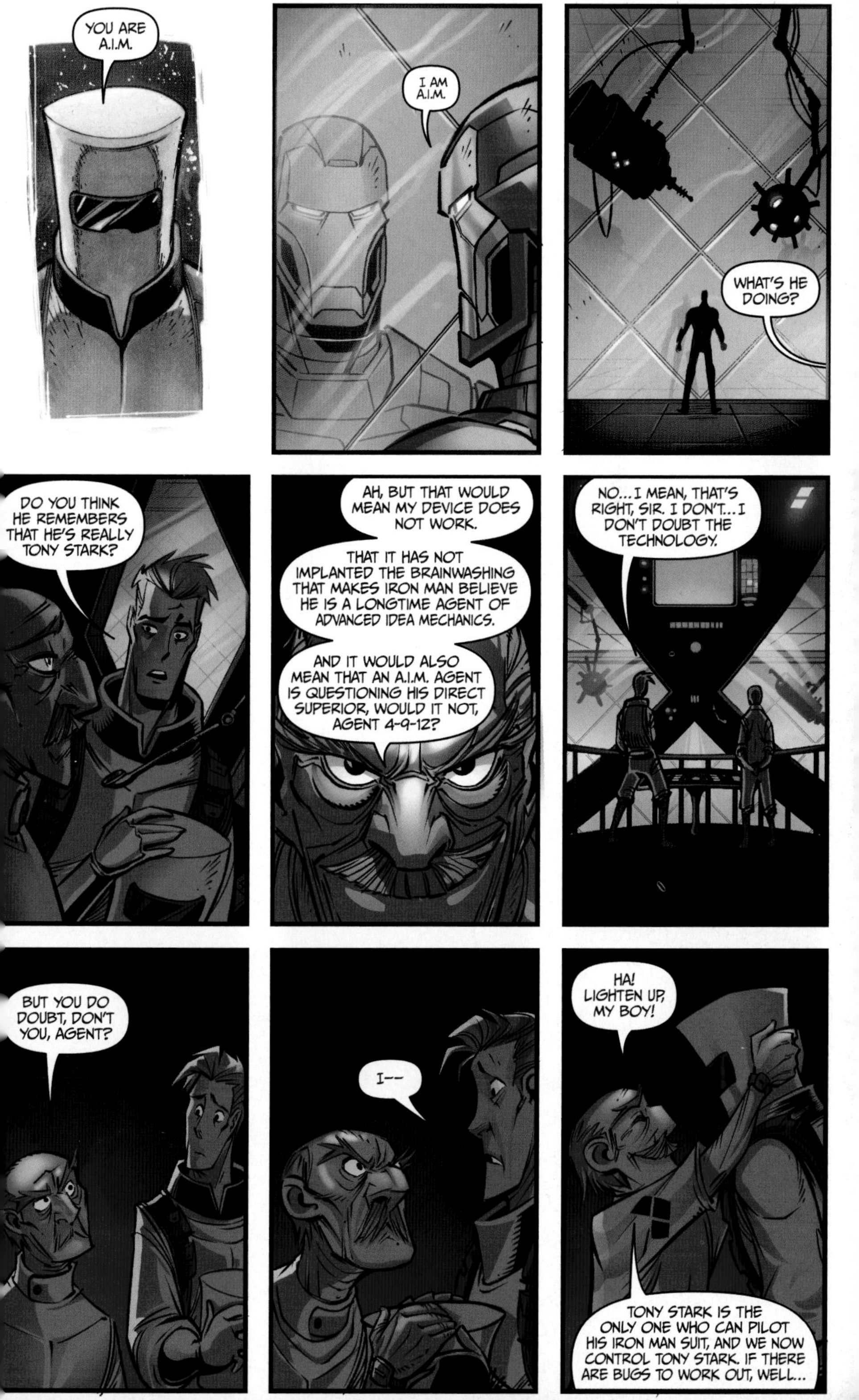
YOU ARE A.I.M.
I AM A.I.M.
WHAT'S HE DOING?
DO YOU THINK HE REMEMBERS THAT HE'S REALLY TONY STARK?
AH, BUT THAT WOULD MEAN MY DEVICE DOES NOT WORK.
THAT IT HAS NOT IMPLANTED THE BRAINWASHING THAT MAKES IRON MAN BELIEVE HE IS A LONGTIME AGENT OF ADVANCED IDEA MECHANICS.
AND IT WOULD ALSO MEAN THAT AN A.I.M. AGENT IS QUESTIONING HIS DIRECT SUPERIOR, WOULD IT NOT, AGENT 4-9-12?
NO... I MEAN, THAT'S RIGHT, SIR. I DON'T... I DON'T DOUBT THE TECHNOLOGY.
BUT YOU DO DOUBT, DON'T YOU, AGENT?
I--
HA! LIGHTEN UP, MY BOY!
TONY STARK IS THE ONLY ONE WHO CAN PILOT HIS IRON MAN SUIT, AND WE NOW CONTROL TONY STARK. IF THERE ARE BUGS TO WORK OUT, WELL...

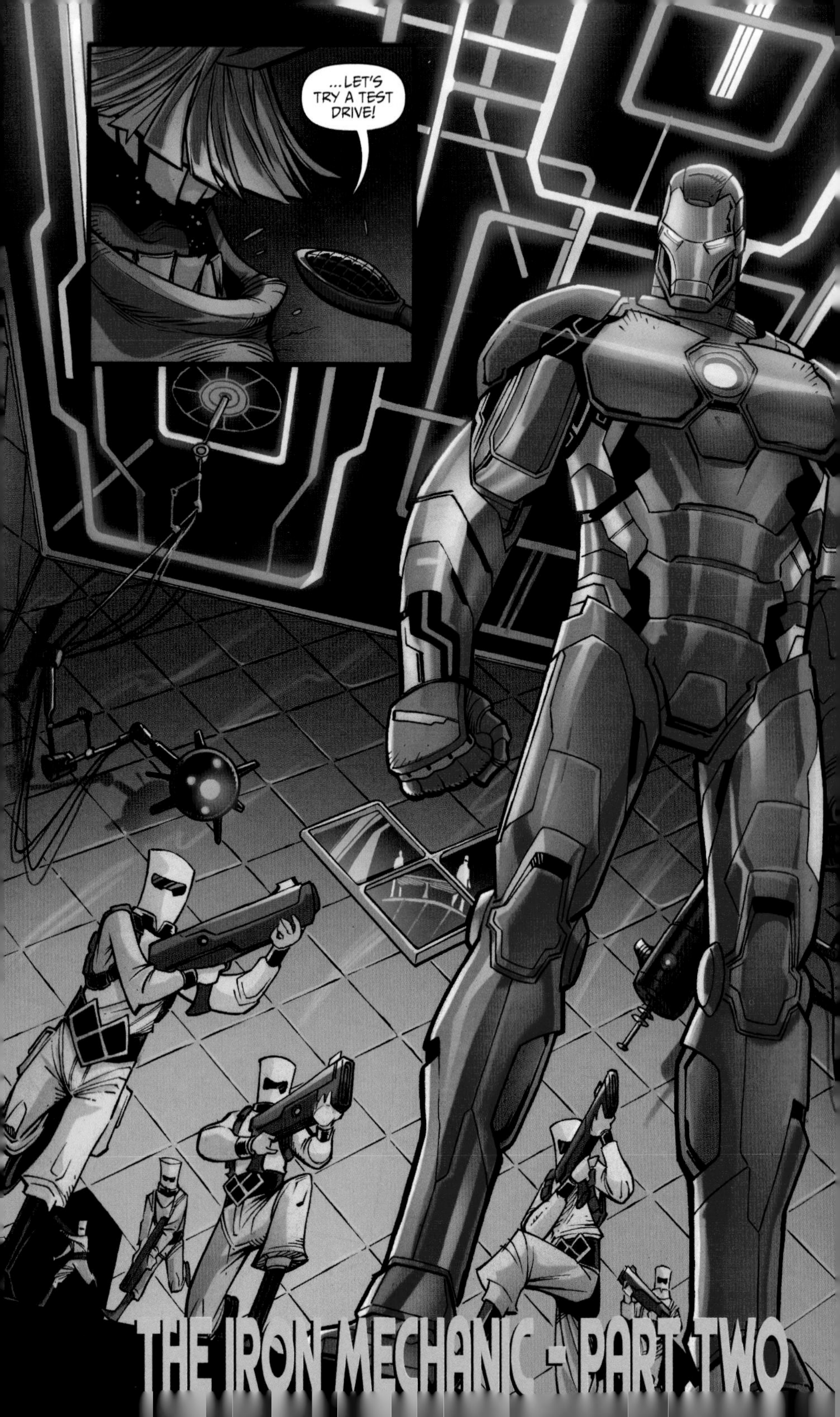
...LET'S TRY A TEST DRIVE!
THE IRON MECHANIC - PART TWO

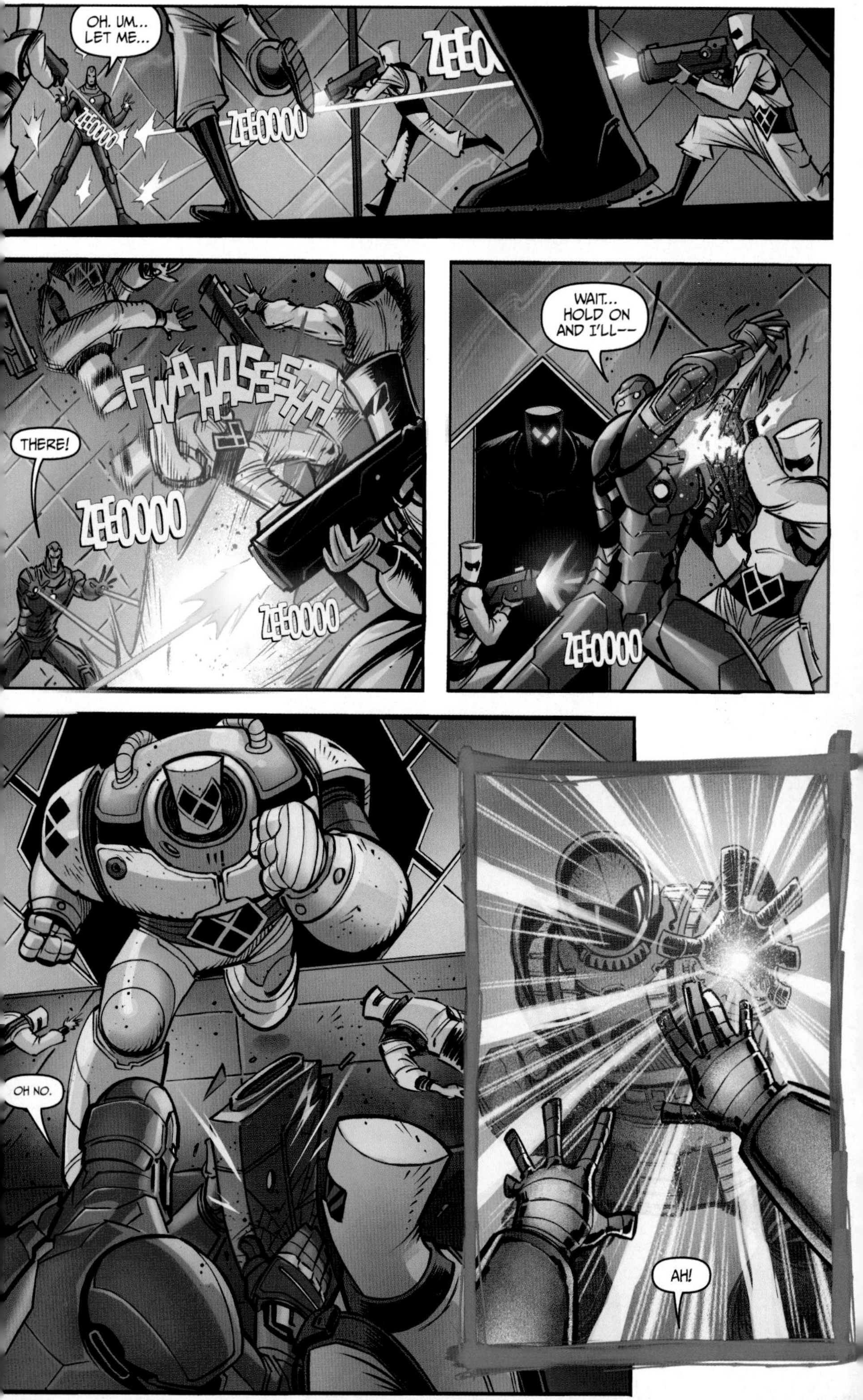
OH. UM... LET ME...
ZEEOOOO
ZEEOOOO
ZEEO
FWAAASSSHH
THERE!
ZEEOOOO
ZEEOOOO
WAIT... HOLD ON AND I'LL--
ZEEOOOO
OH NO.
AH!

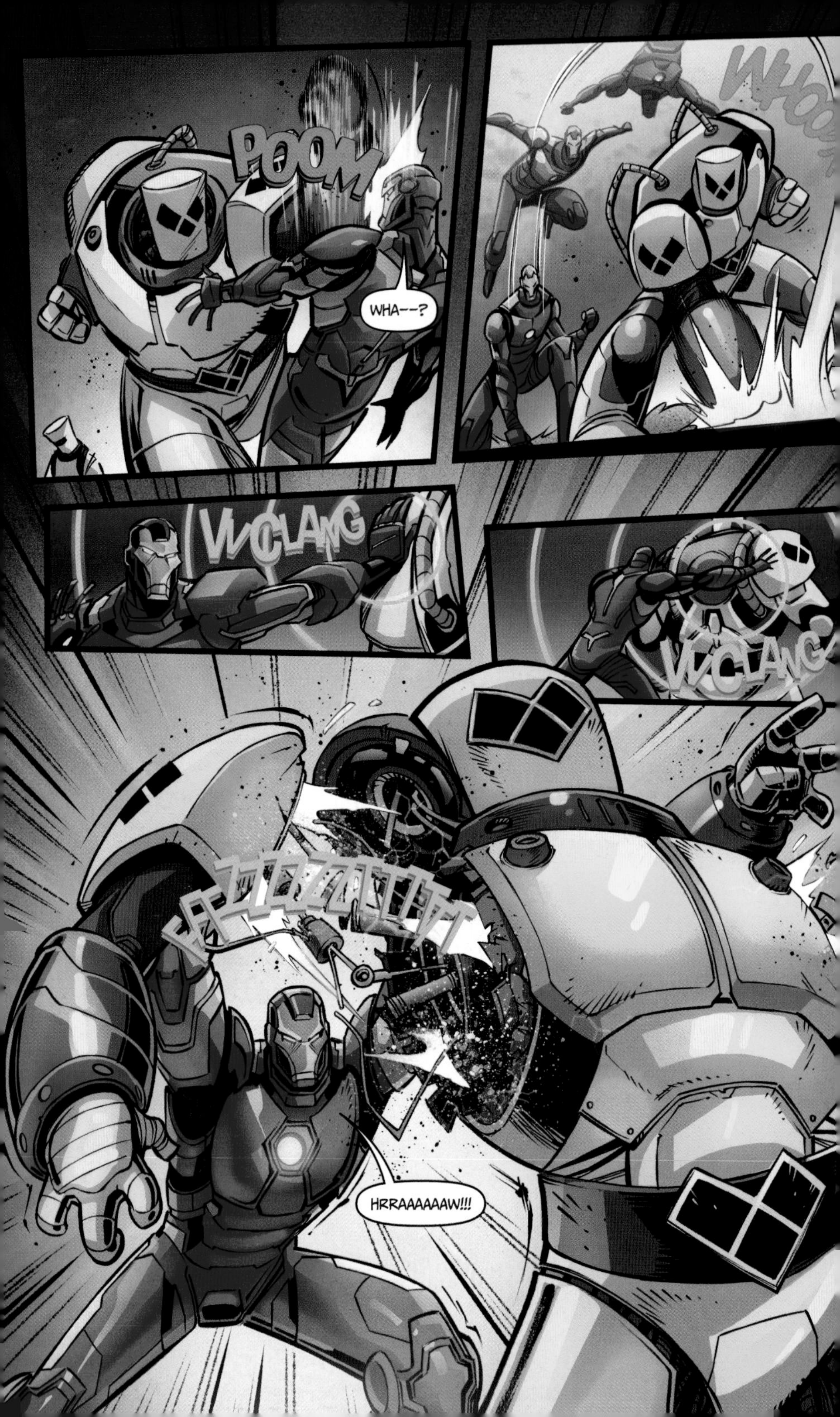

POOM
WHA--?
WHOOM
VVCLANG
VVCLANG
FFZZZZTTTT
HRRAAAAAAW!!!

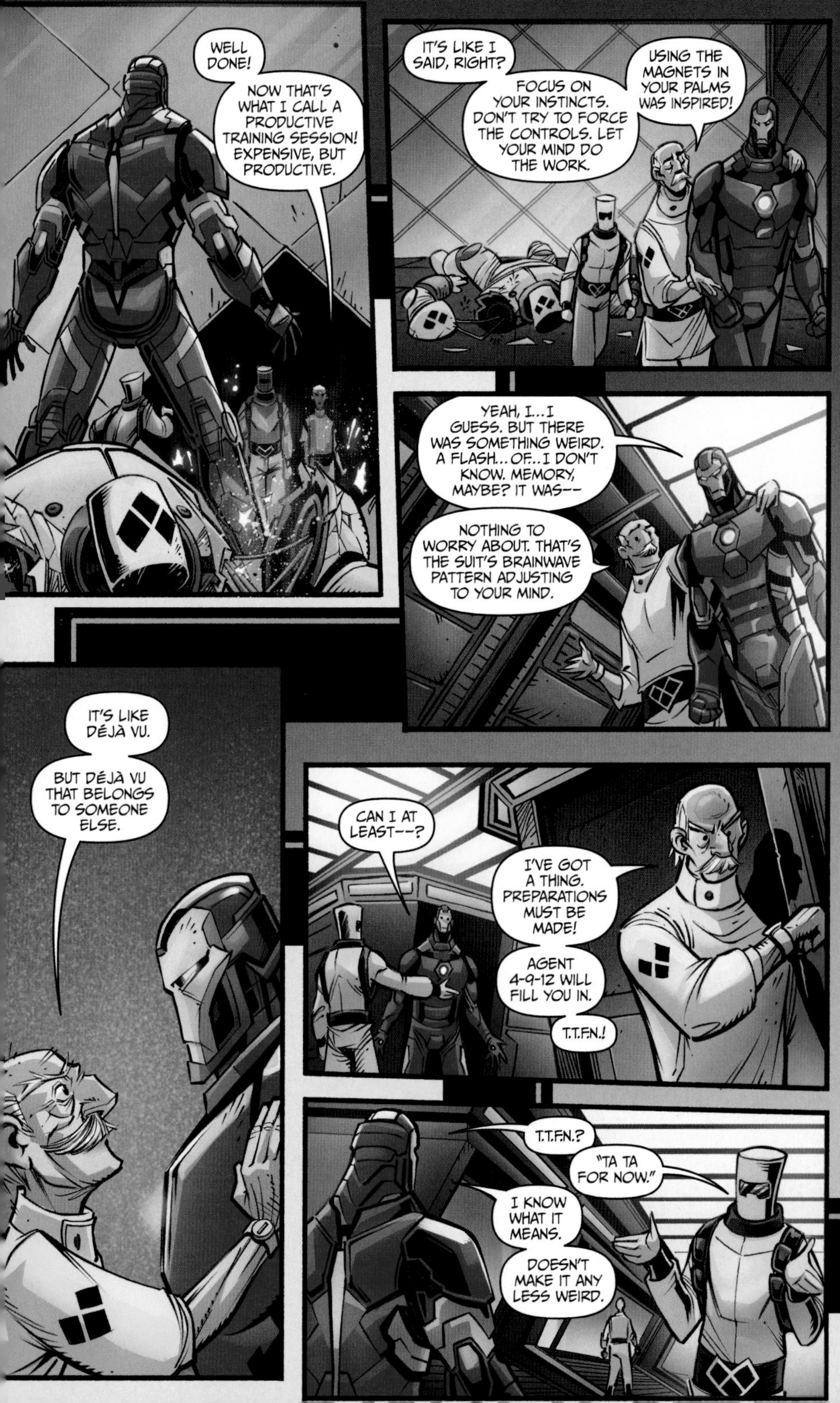
WELL DONE!
NOW THAT'S WHAT I CALL A PRODUCTIVE TRAINING SESSION! EXPENSIVE, BUT PRODUCTIVE.
IT'S LIKE I SAID, RIGHT?
FOCUS ON YOUR INSTINCTS. DON'T TRY TO FORCE THE CONTROLS. LET YOUR MIND DO THE WORK.
USING THE MAGNETS IN YOUR PALMS WAS INSPIRED!
YEAH, I...I GUESS. BUT THERE WAS SOMETHING WEIRD. A FLASH...OF...I DON'T KNOW. MEMORY, MAYBE? IT WAS--
NOTHING TO WORRY ABOUT. THAT'S THE SUIT'S BRAINWAVE PATTERN ADJUSTING TO YOUR MIND.
IT'S LIKE DÉJÀ VU.
BUT DÉJÀ VU THAT BELONGS TO SOMEONE ELSE.
CAN I AT LEAST--?
I'VE GOT A THING. PREPARATIONS MUST BE MADE!
AGENT 4-9-12 WILL FILL YOU IN.
T.T.F.N.!
T.T.F.N.?
"TA TA FOR NOW."
I KNOW WHAT IT MEANS.
DOESN'T MAKE IT ANY LESS WEIRD.

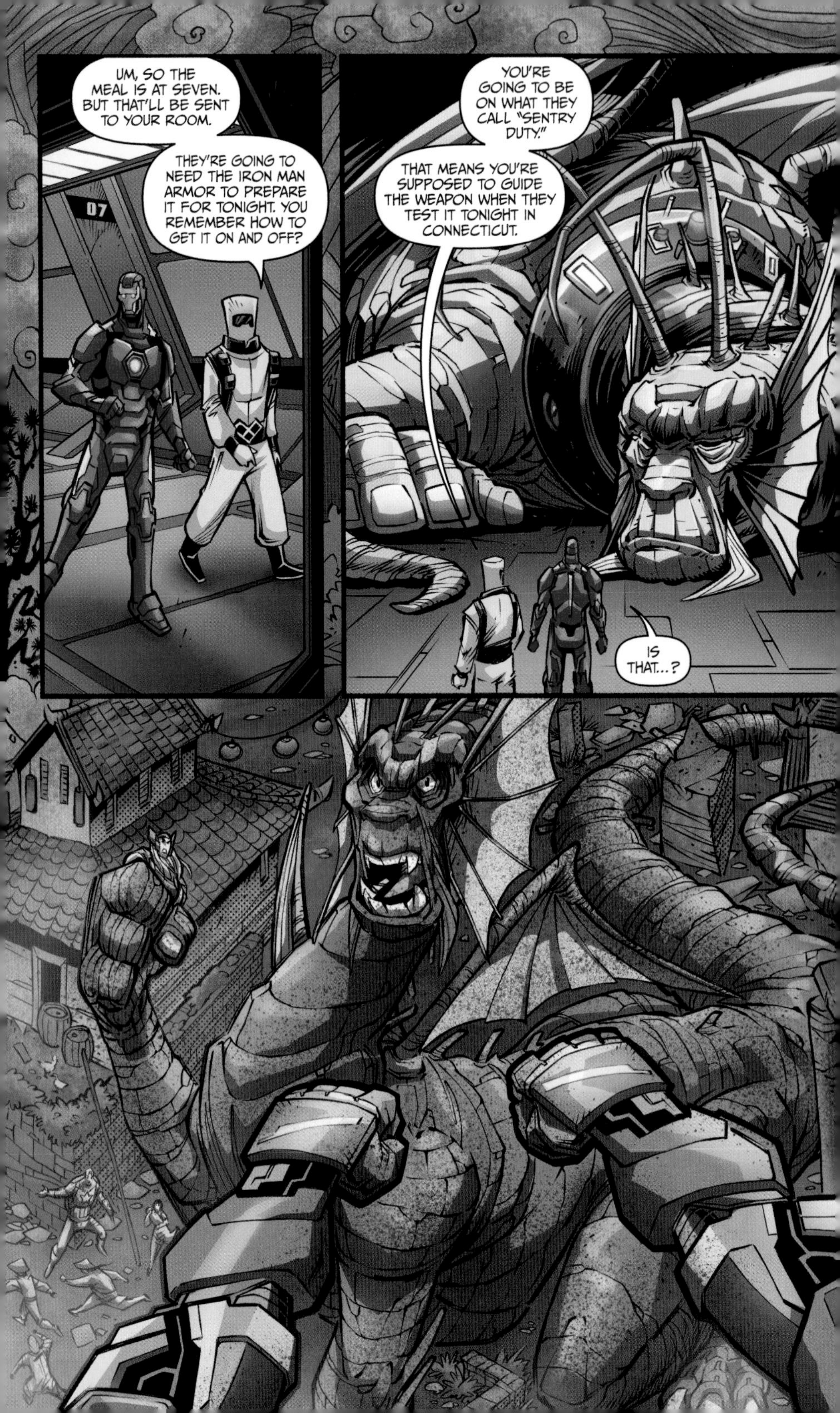
UM, SO THE MEAL IS AT SEVEN. BUT THAT'LL BE SENT TO YOUR ROOM.
THEY'RE GOING TO NEED THE IRON MAN ARMOR TO PREPARE IT FOR TONIGHT. YOU REMEMBER HOW TO GET IT ON AND OFF?
07
YOU'RE GOING TO BE ON WHAT THEY CALL "SENTRY DUTY."
THAT MEANS YOU'RE SUPPOSED TO GUIDE THE WEAPON WHEN THEY TEST IT TONIGHT IN CONNECTICUT.
IS THAT...?

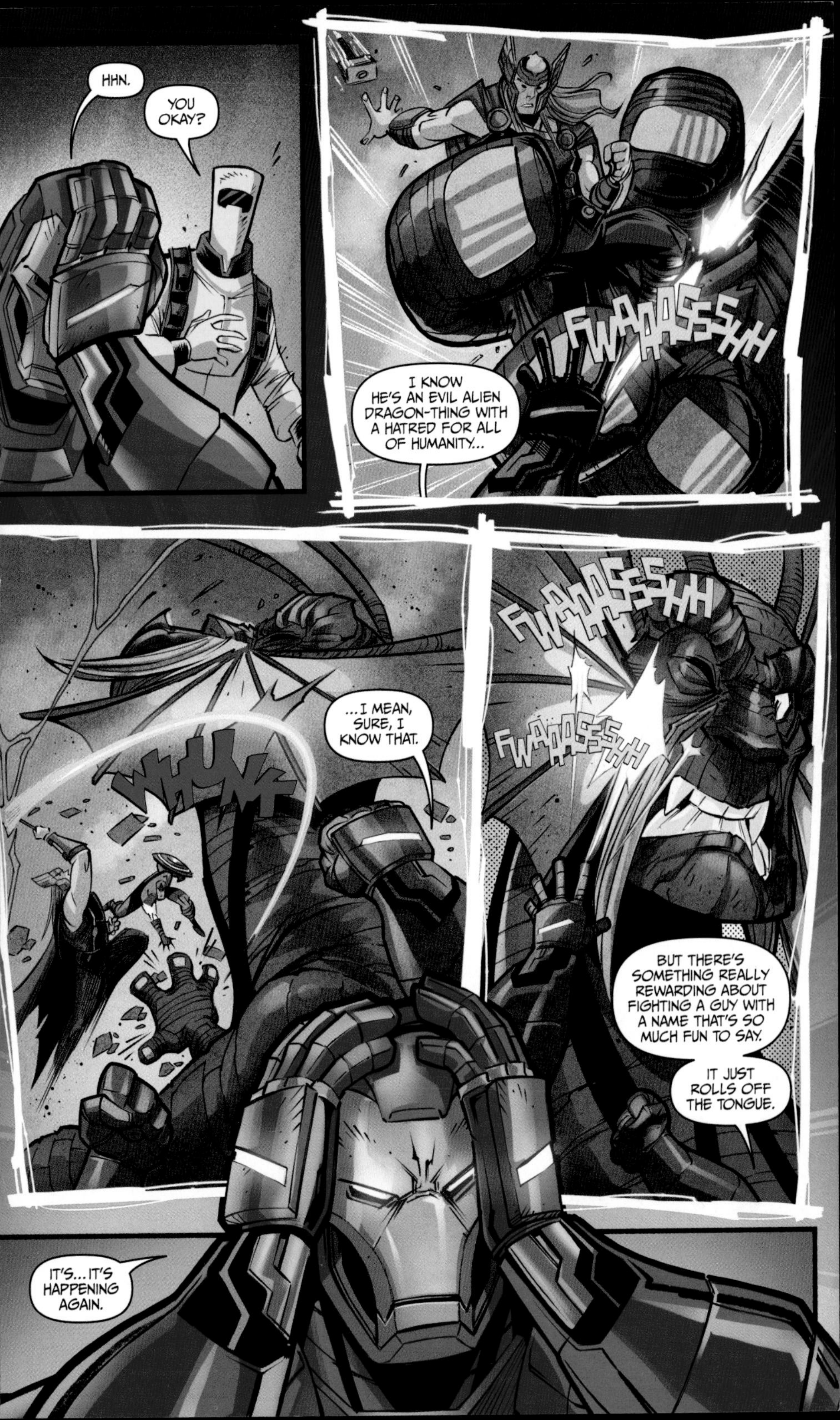
HHN.
YOU OKAY?
FWAAASSSHH
I KNOW HE'S AN EVIL ALIEN DRAGON-THING WITH A HATRED FOR ALL OF HUMANITY...
WHUNK
...I MEAN, SURE, I KNOW THAT.
FWAAASSSHH
FWAAASSSHH
BUT THERE'S SOMETHING REALLY REWARDING ABOUT FIGHTING A GUY WITH A NAME THAT'S SO MUCH FUN TO SAY.
IT JUST ROLLS OFF THE TONGUE.
IT'S... IT'S HAPPENING AGAIN.

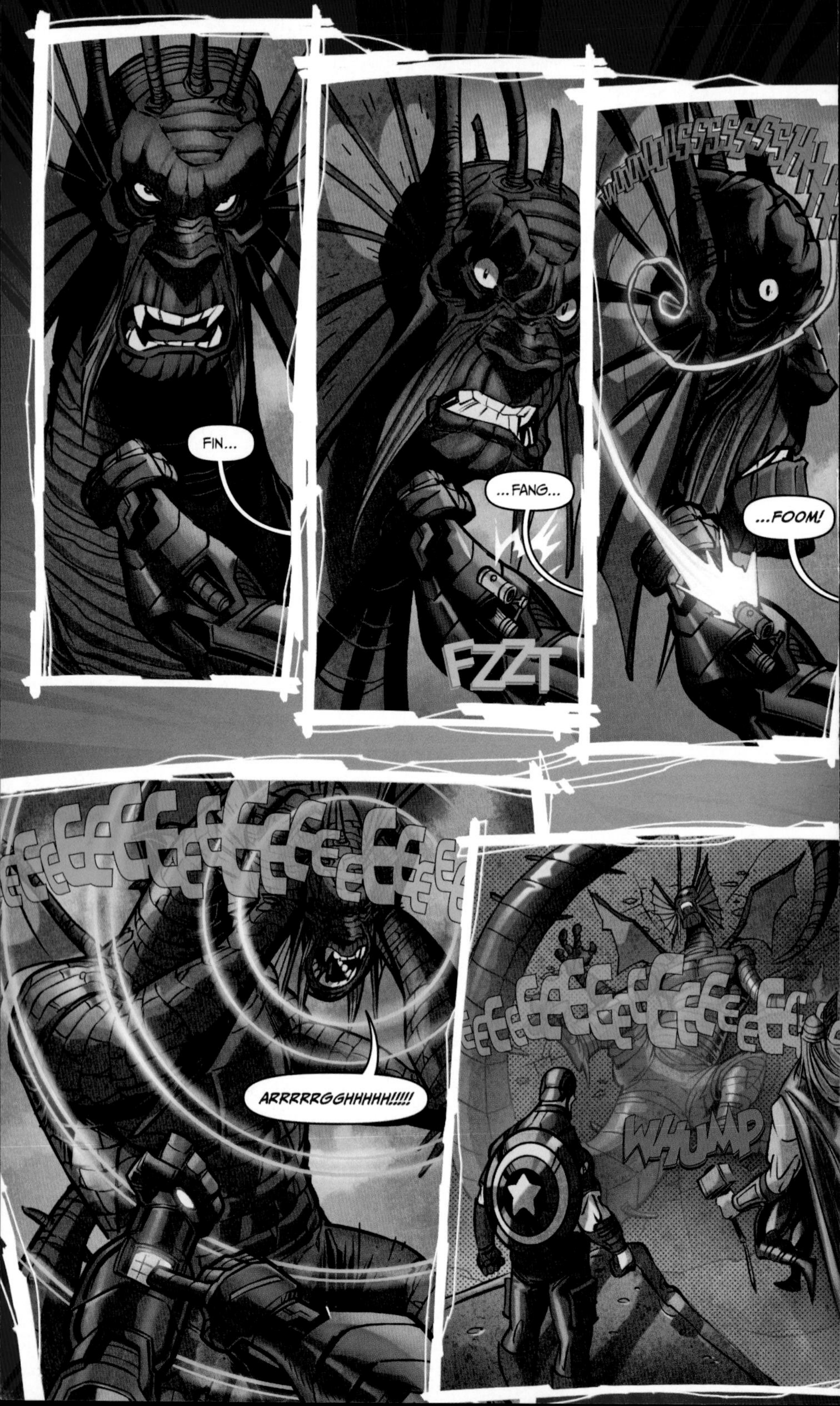
FIN...
...FANG...
FZZT
WHOOSSSSSSSSH
...FOOM!
EEEEEEEEEEEEEEEEEE
ARRRRRGGHHHHH!!!!!
EEEEEEEEEEEEEEEEEE
WHUMP

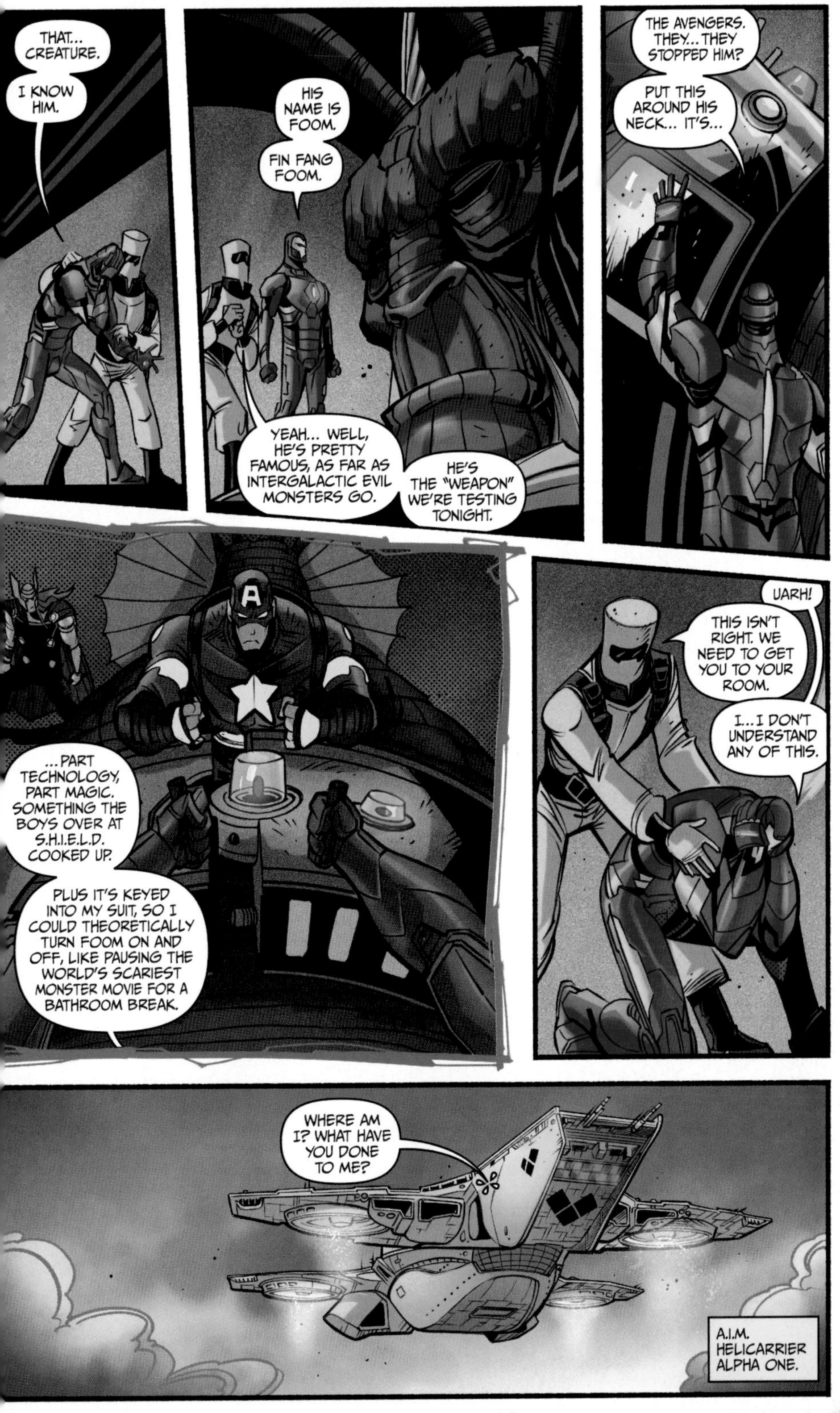
THAT... CREATURE.
I KNOW HIM.
HIS NAME IS FOOM.
FIN FANG FOOM.
YEAH... WELL, HE'S PRETTY FAMOUS, AS FAR AS INTERGALACTIC EVIL MONSTERS GO.
HE'S THE "WEAPON" WE'RE TESTING TONIGHT.
THE AVENGERS. THEY... THEY STOPPED HIM?
PUT THIS AROUND HIS NECK... IT'S...
...PART TECHNOLOGY, PART MAGIC. SOMETHING THE BOYS OVER AT S.H.I.E.L.D. COOKED UP.
PLUS IT'S KEYED INTO MY SUIT, SO I COULD THEORETICALLY TURN FOOM ON AND OFF, LIKE PAUSING THE WORLD'S SCARIEST MONSTER MOVIE FOR A BATHROOM BREAK.
UARH!
THIS ISN'T RIGHT. WE NEED TO GET YOU TO YOUR ROOM.
I...I DON'T UNDERSTAND ANY OF THIS.
WHERE AM I? WHAT HAVE YOU DONE TO ME?
A.I.M. HELICARRIER ALPHA ONE.

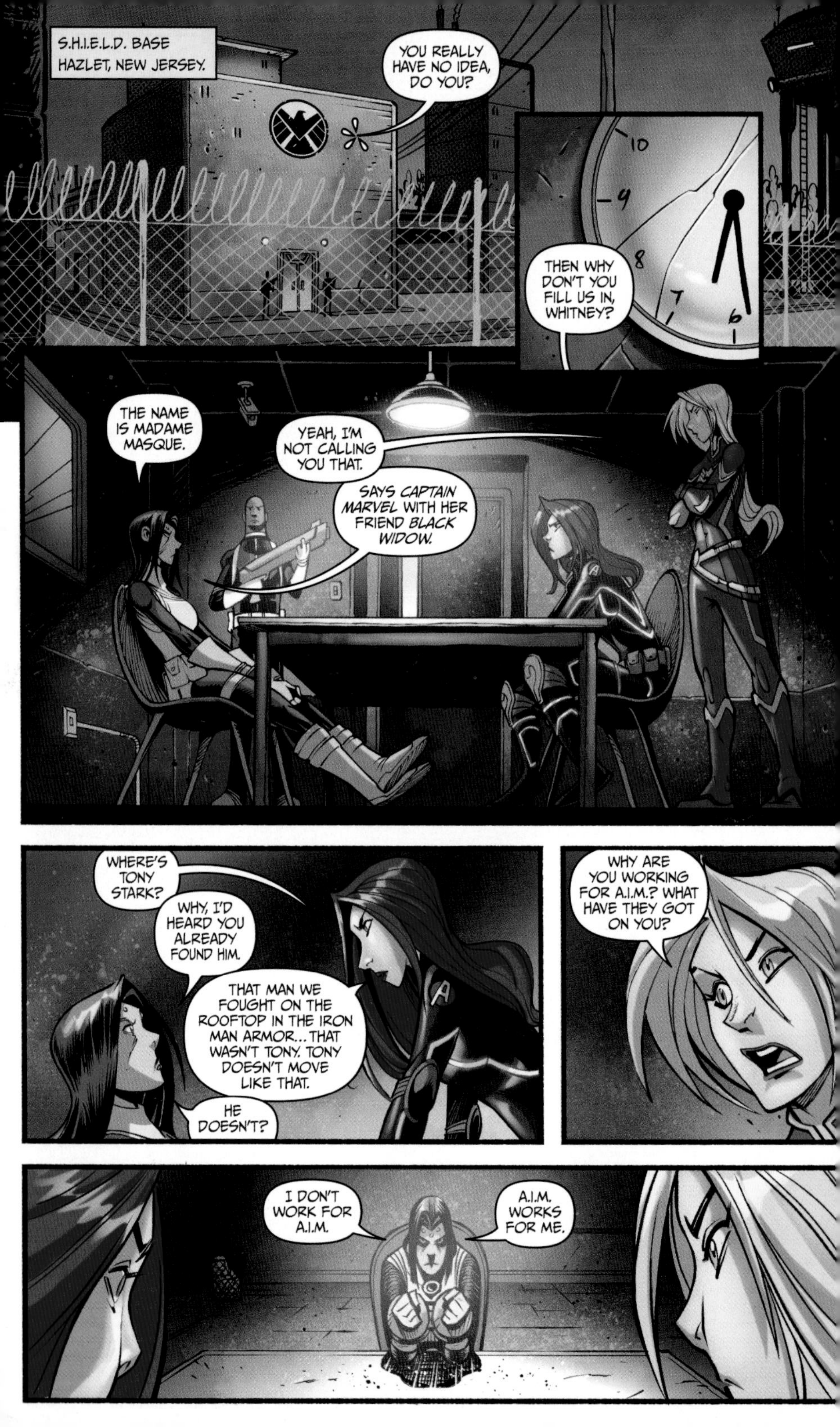
S.H.I.E.L.D. BASE
HAZLET, NEW JERSEY.
YOU REALLY HAVE NO IDEA, DO YOU?
THEN WHY DON'T YOU FILL US IN, WHITNEY?
THE NAME IS MADAME MASQUE.
YEAH, I'M NOT CALLING YOU THAT.
SAYS *CAPTAIN MARVEL* WITH HER FRIEND *BLACK WIDOW.*
WHERE'S TONY STARK?
WHY, I'D HEARD YOU ALREADY FOUND HIM.
THAT MAN WE FOUGHT ON THE ROOFTOP IN THE IRON MAN ARMOR... THAT WASN'T TONY. TONY DOESN'T MOVE LIKE THAT.
HE DOESN'T?
WHY ARE YOU WORKING FOR A.I.M.? WHAT HAVE THEY GOT ON YOU?
I DON'T WORK FOR A.I.M.
A.I.M. WORKS FOR ME.

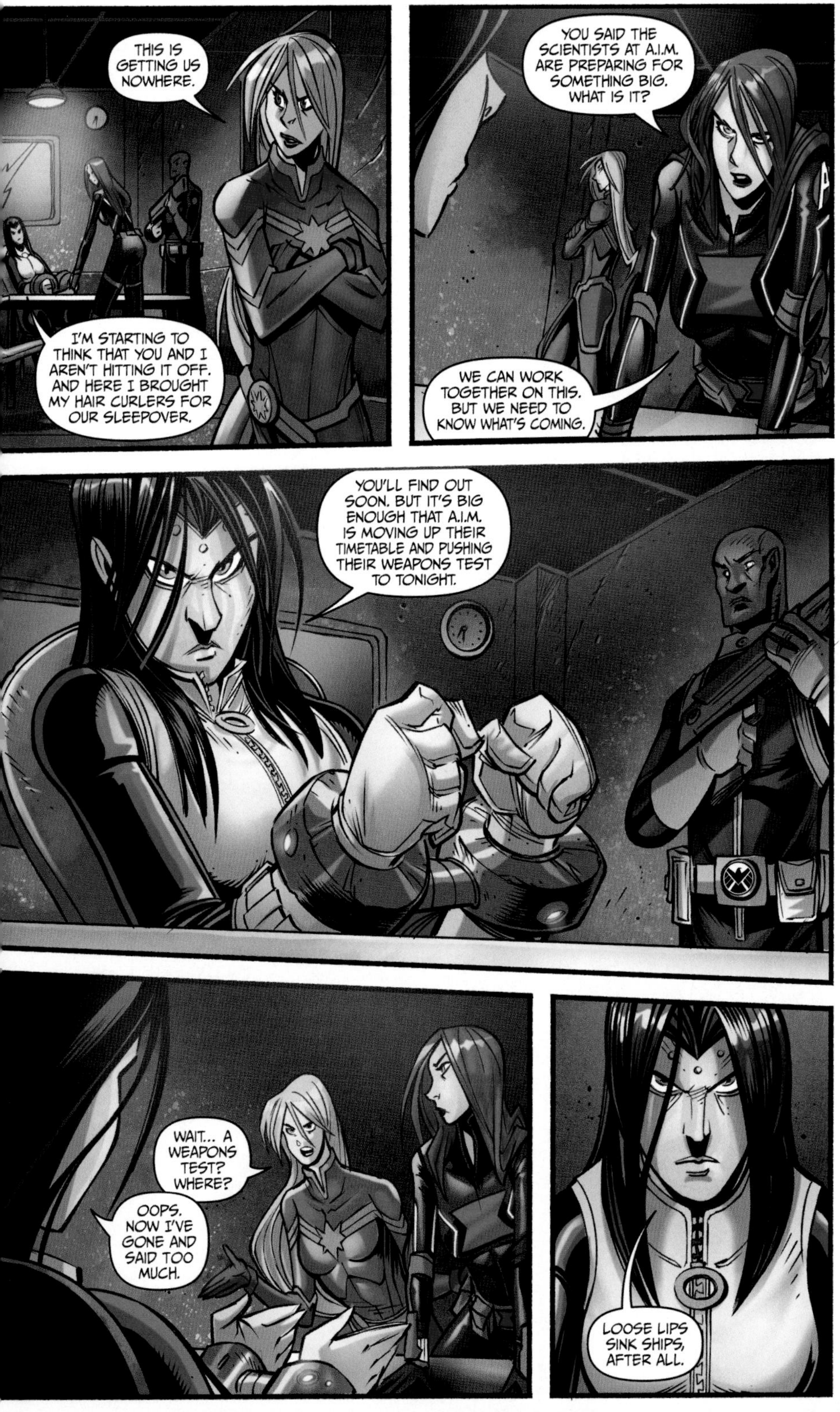
THIS IS GETTING US NOWHERE.
I'M STARTING TO THINK THAT YOU AND I AREN'T HITTING IT OFF. AND HERE I BROUGHT MY HAIR CURLERS FOR OUR SLEEPOVER.
YOU SAID THE SCIENTISTS AT A.I.M. ARE PREPARING FOR SOMETHING BIG. WHAT IS IT?
WE CAN WORK TOGETHER ON THIS. BUT WE NEED TO KNOW WHAT'S COMING.
YOU'LL FIND OUT SOON. BUT IT'S BIG ENOUGH THAT A.I.M. IS MOVING UP THEIR TIMETABLE AND PUSHING THEIR WEAPONS TEST TO TONIGHT.
WAIT... A WEAPONS TEST? WHERE?
OOPS. NOW I'VE GONE AND SAID TOO MUCH.
LOOSE LIPS SINK SHIPS, AFTER ALL.

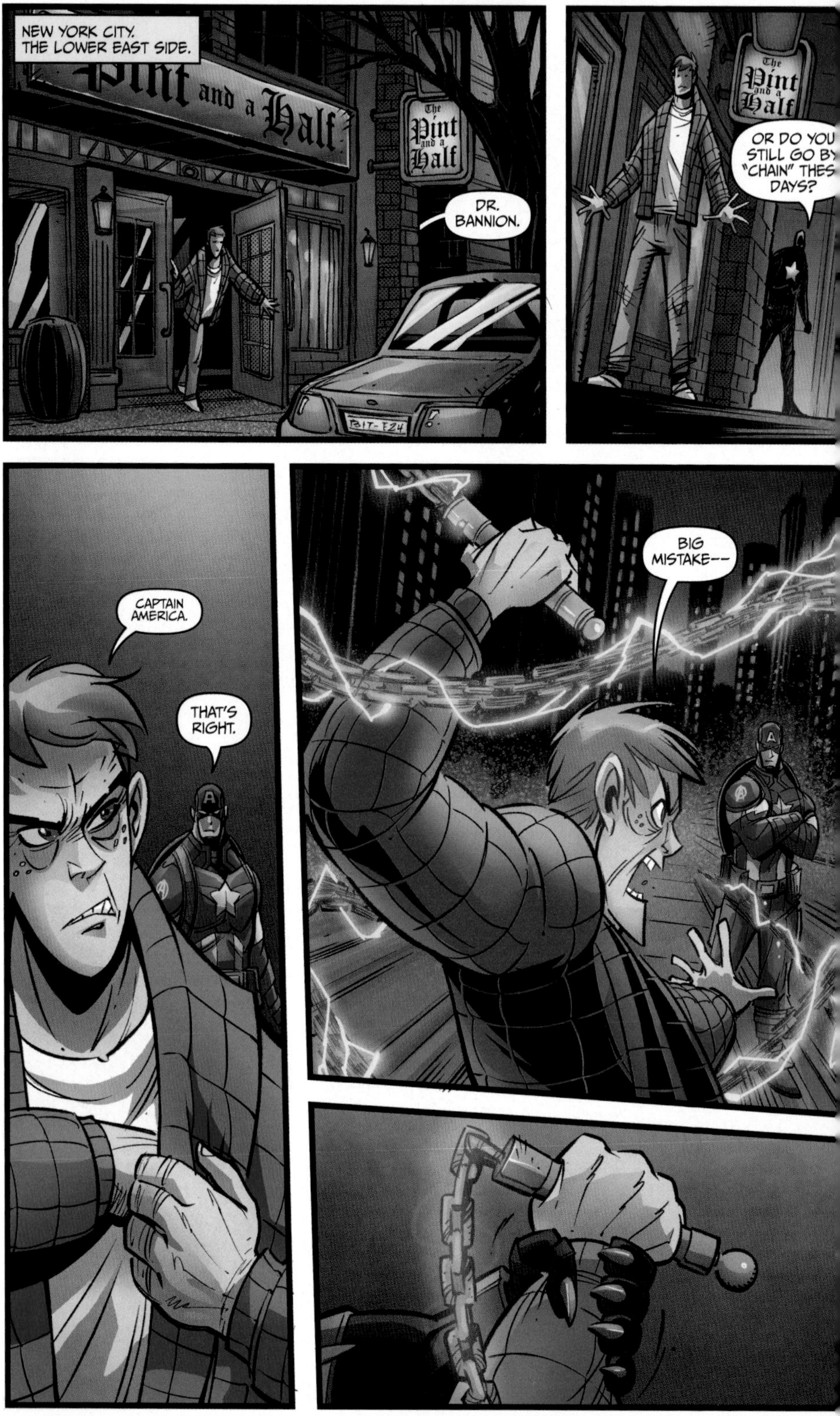
NEW YORK CITY.
THE LOWER EAST SIDE.
The Pint and a Half
DR. BANNION.
OR DO YOU STILL GO BY "CHAIN" THES DAYS?
CAPTAIN AMERICA.
THAT'S RIGHT.
BIG MISTAKE--

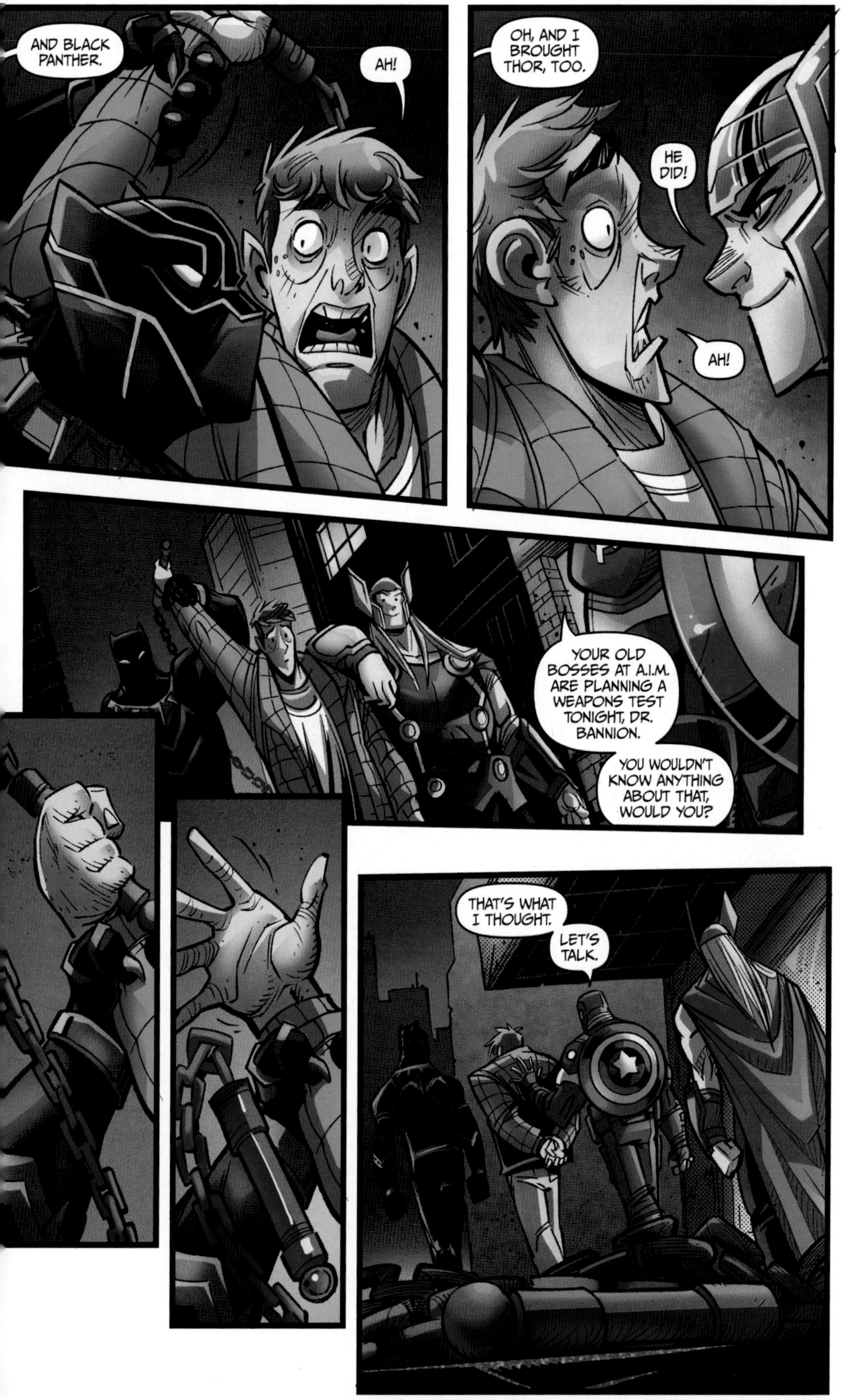
AND BLACK PANTHER.
AH!
OH, AND I BROUGHT THOR, TOO.
HE DID!
AH!
YOUR OLD BOSSES AT A.I.M. ARE PLANNING A WEAPONS TEST TONIGHT, DR. BANNION.
YOU WOULDN'T KNOW ANYTHING ABOUT THAT, WOULD YOU?
THAT'S WHAT I THOUGHT.
LET'S TALK.

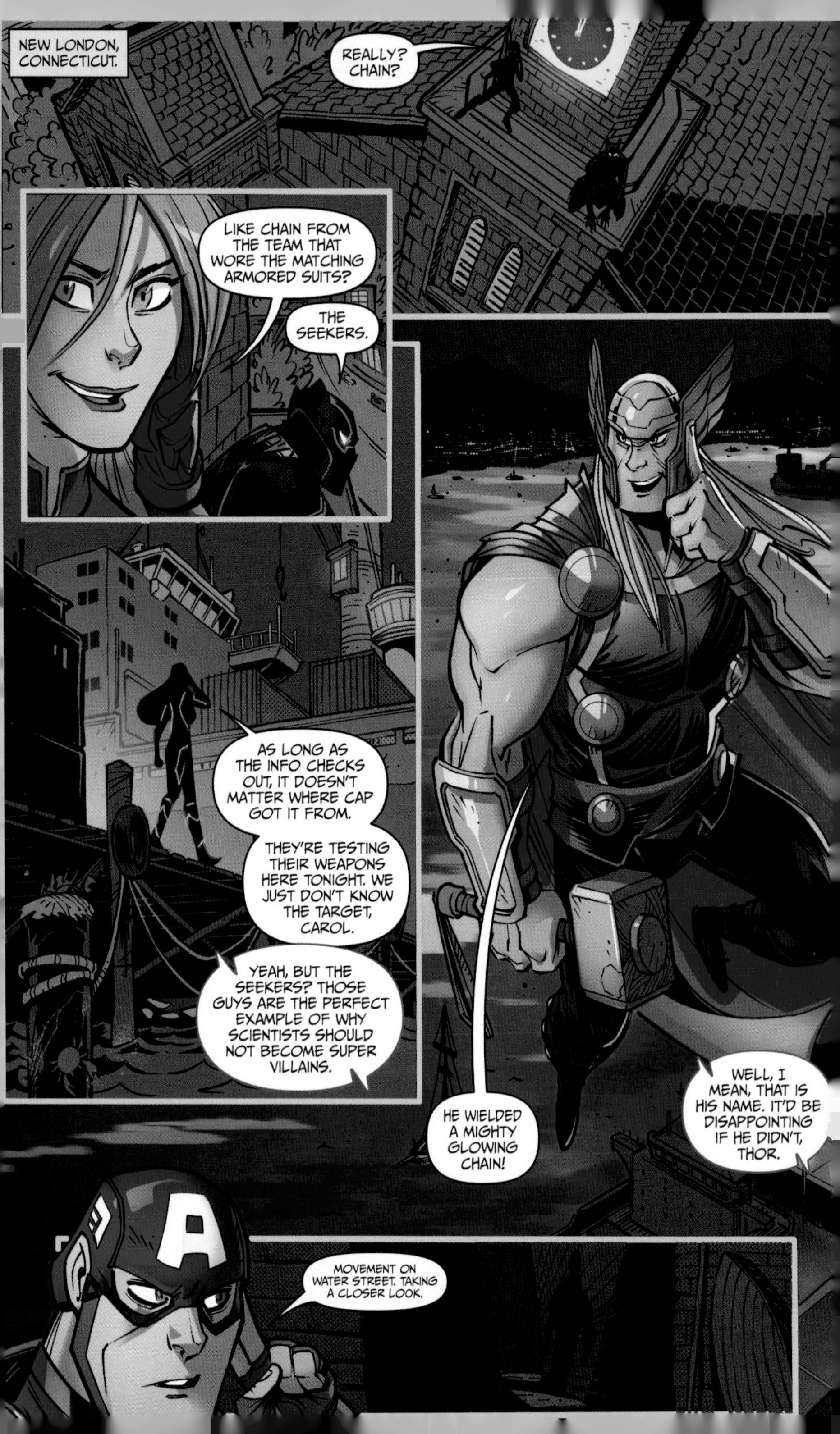

NEW LONDON, CONNECTICUT.
REALLY? CHAIN?
LIKE CHAIN FROM THE TEAM THAT WORE THE MATCHING ARMORED SUITS?
THE SEEKERS.
AS LONG AS THE INFO CHECKS OUT, IT DOESN'T MATTER WHERE CAP GOT IT FROM.
THEY'RE TESTING THEIR WEAPONS HERE TONIGHT. WE JUST DON'T KNOW THE TARGET, CAROL.
YEAH, BUT THE SEEKERS? THOSE GUYS ARE THE PERFECT EXAMPLE OF WHY SCIENTISTS SHOULD NOT BECOME SUPER VILLAINS.
HE WIELDED A MIGHTY GLOWING CHAIN!
WELL, I MEAN, THAT IS HIS NAME. IT'D BE DISAPPOINTING IF HE DIDN'T, THOR.
MOVEMENT ON WATER STREET. TAKING A CLOSER LOOK.

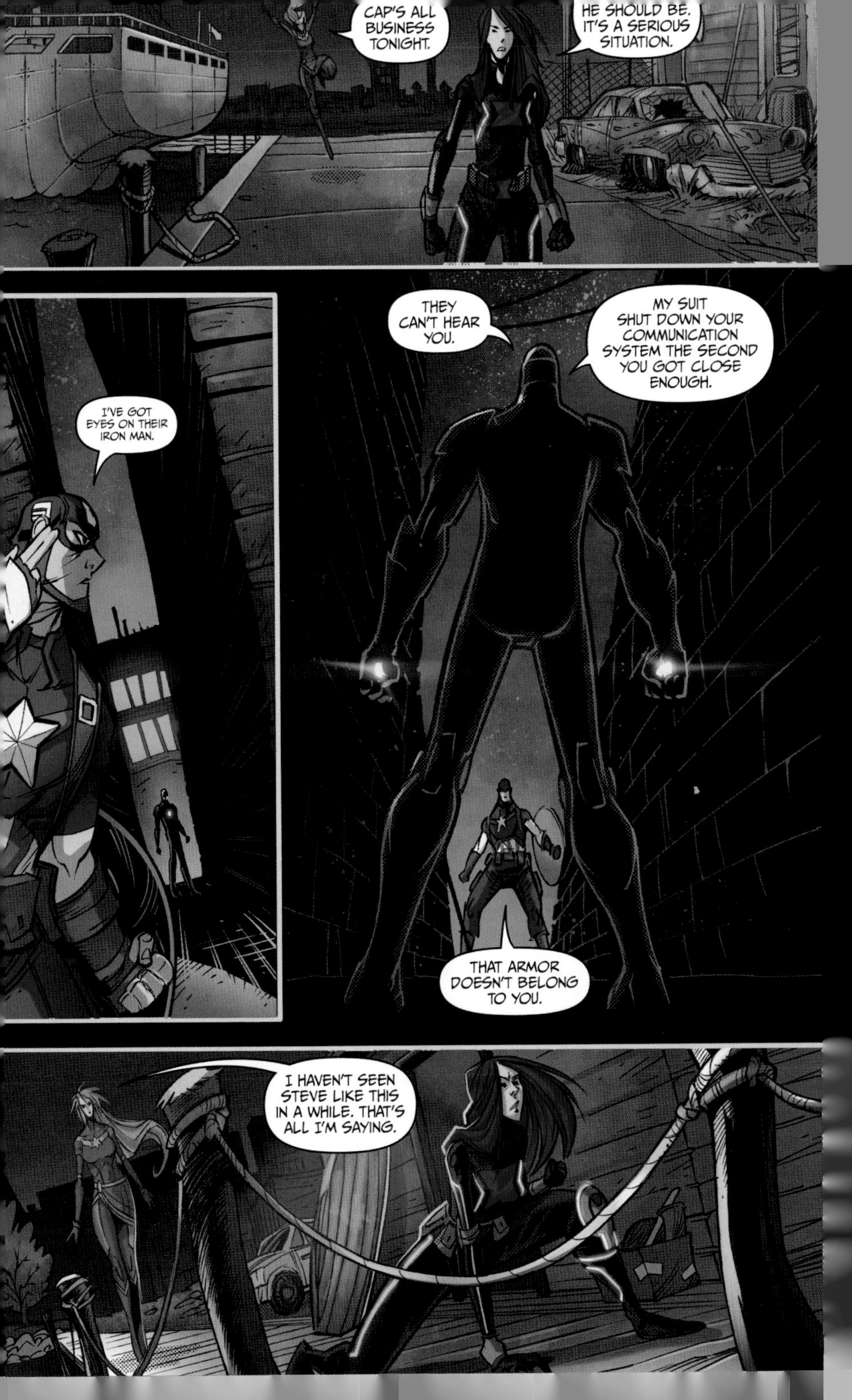
CAP'S ALL BUSINESS TONIGHT.
HE SHOULD BE. IT'S A SERIOUS SITUATION.
I'VE GOT EYES ON THEIR IRON MAN.
THEY CAN'T HEAR YOU.
MY SUIT SHUT DOWN YOUR COMMUNICATION SYSTEM THE SECOND YOU GOT CLOSE ENOUGH.
THAT ARMOR DOESN'T BELONG TO YOU.
I HAVEN'T SEEN STEVE LIKE THIS IN A WHILE. THAT'S ALL I'M SAYING.

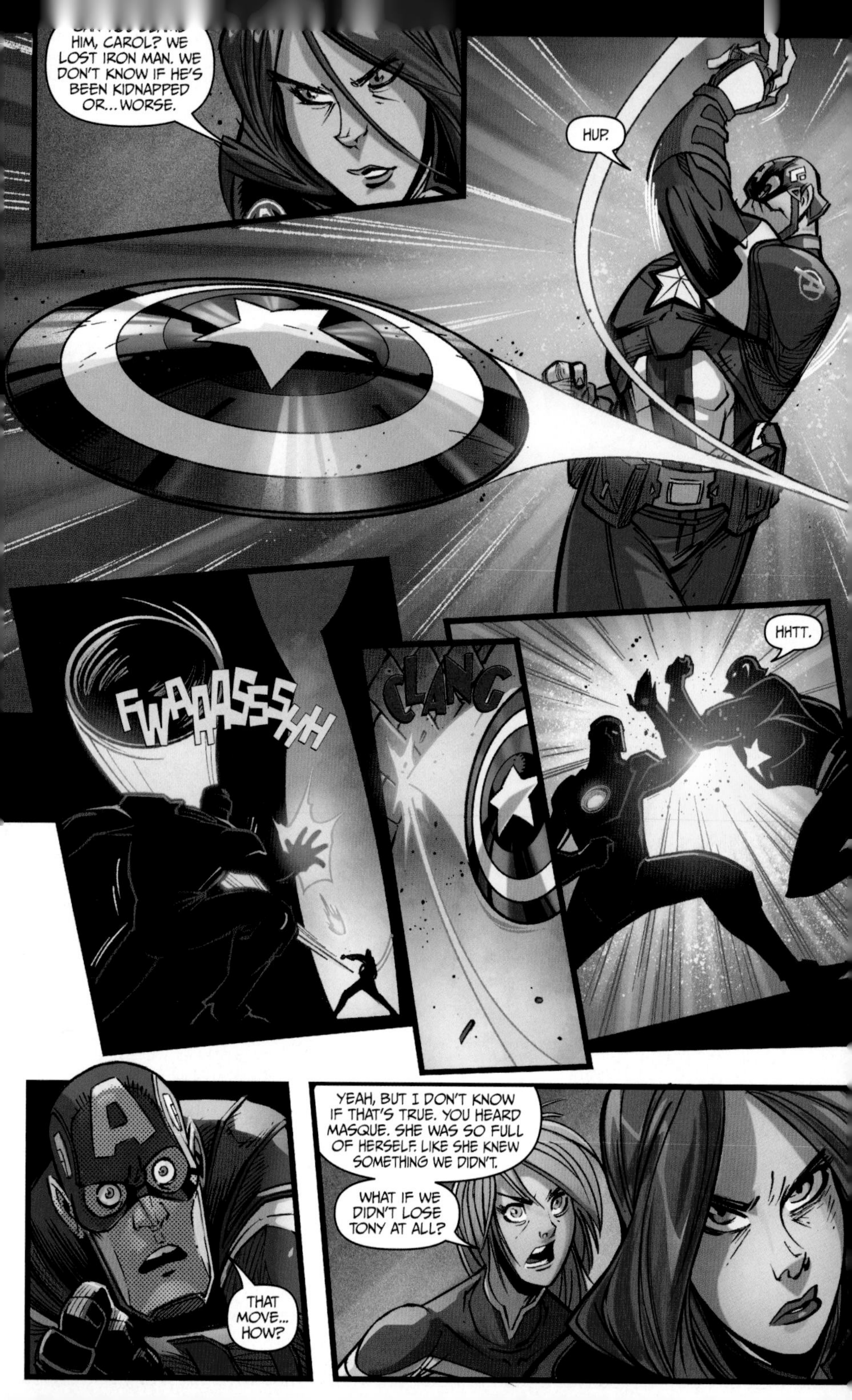

HIM, CAROL? WE LOST IRON MAN. WE DON'T KNOW IF HE'S BEEN KIDNAPPED OR...WORSE.
HUP.
FWAAASSSHH
CLANG
HHTT.
THAT MOVE... HOW?
YEAH, BUT I DON'T KNOW IF THAT'S TRUE. YOU HEARD MASQUE. SHE WAS SO FULL OF HERSELF. LIKE SHE KNEW SOMETHING WE DIDN'T.
WHAT IF WE DIDN'T LOSE TONY AT ALL?

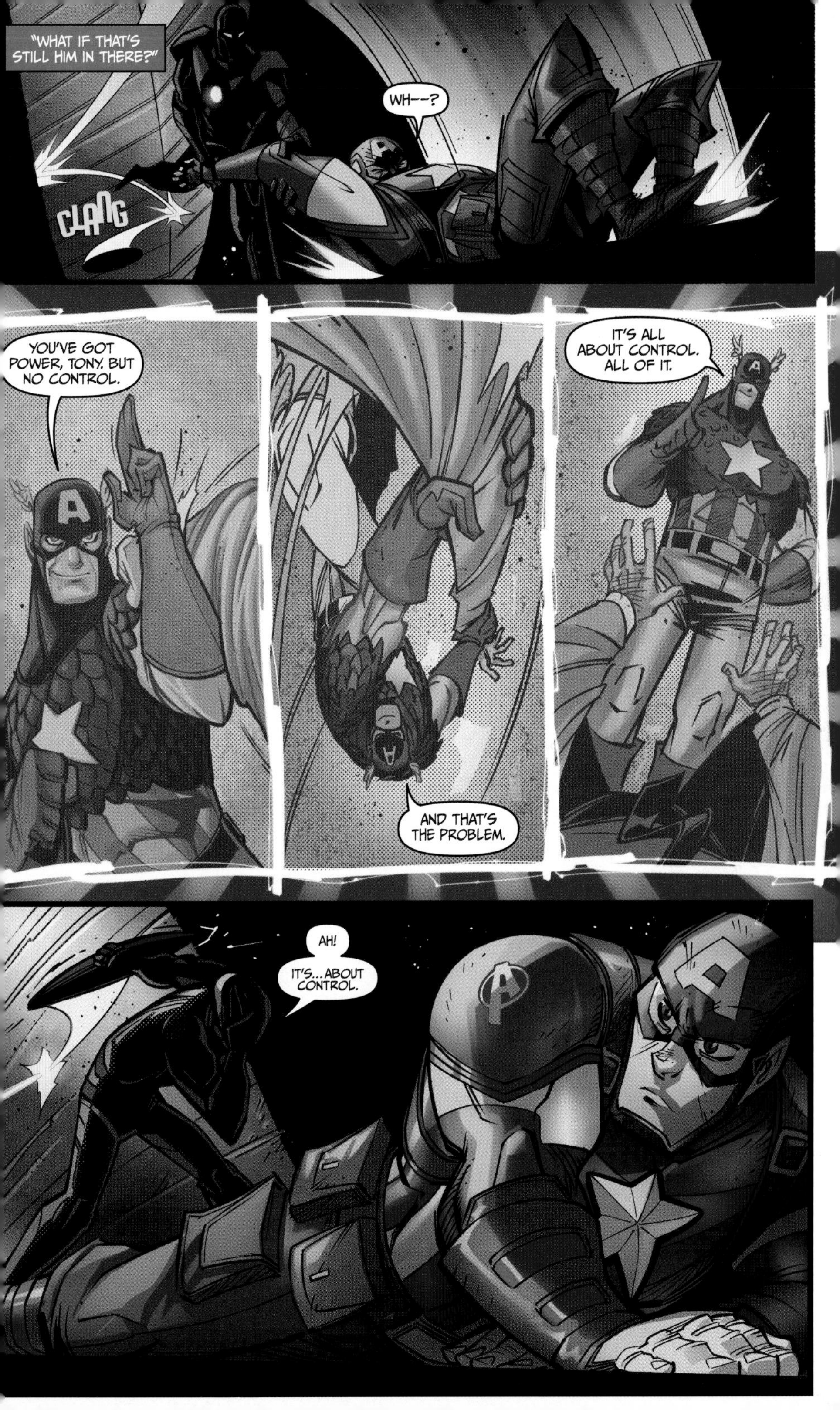
"WHAT IF THAT'S STILL HIM IN THERE?"
WH--?
CLANG
YOU'VE GOT POWER, TONY. BUT NO CONTROL.
AND THAT'S THE PROBLEM.
IT'S ALL ABOUT CONTROL. ALL OF IT.
AH!
IT'S...ABOUT CONTROL.

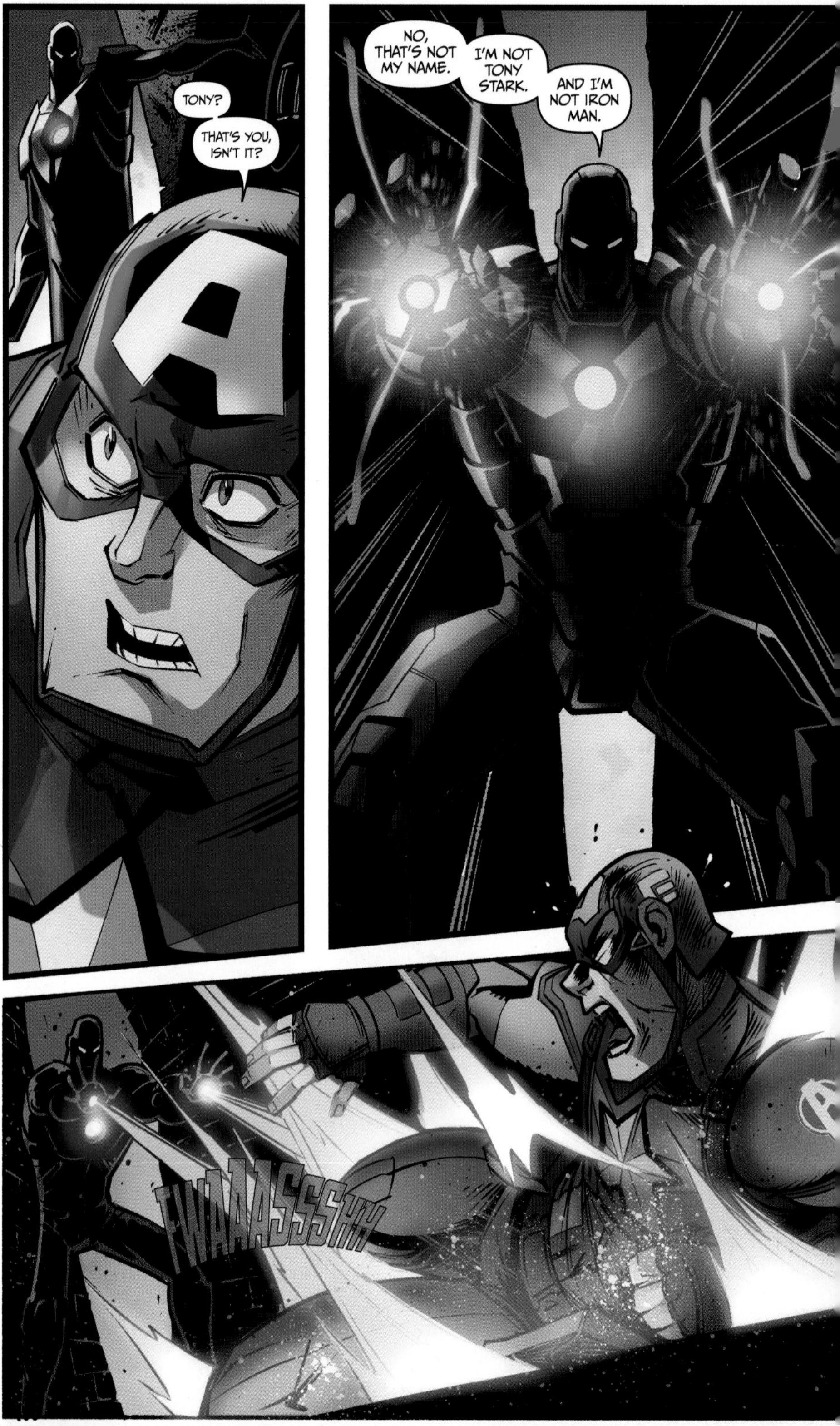
TONY?
THAT'S YOU, ISN'T IT?
NO, THAT'S NOT MY NAME.
I'M NOT TONY STARK.
AND I'M NOT IRON MAN.
FWAAASSSHH

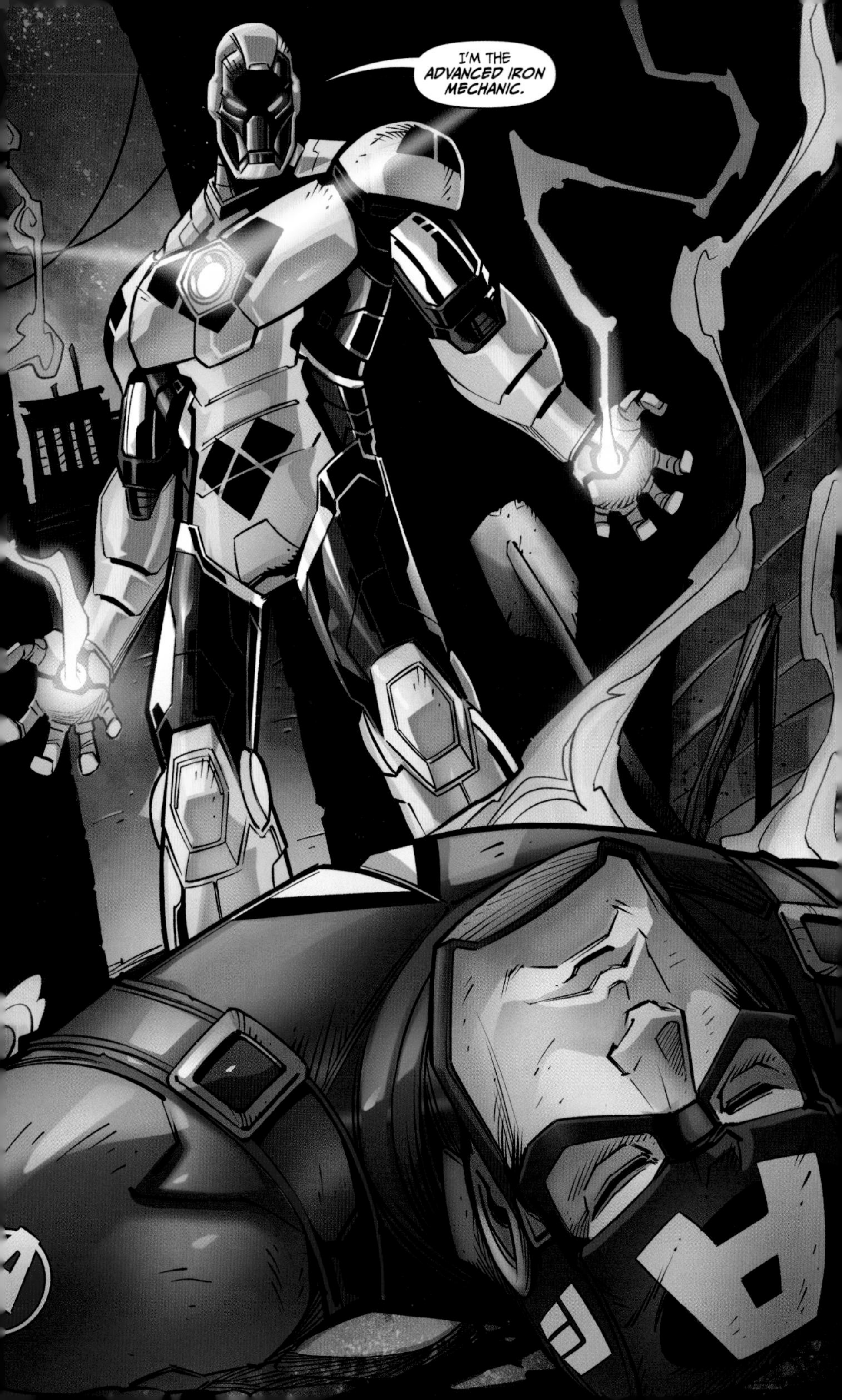
I'M THE ADVANCED IRON MECHANIC.

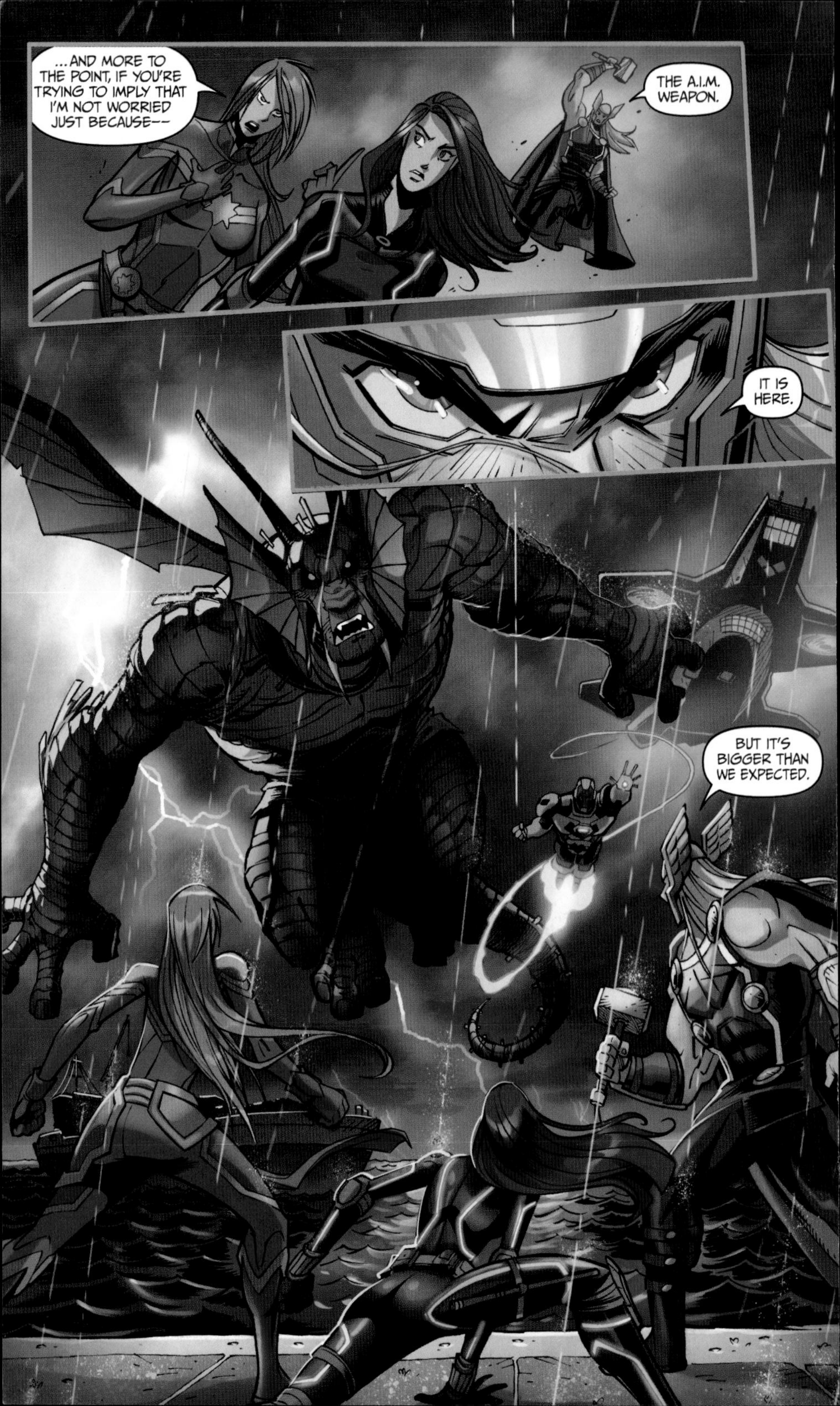
...AND MORE TO THE POINT, IF YOU'RE TRYING TO IMPLY THAT I'M NOT WORRIED JUST BECAUSE--
THE A.I.M. WEAPON.
IT IS HERE.
BUT IT'S BIGGER THAN WE EXPECTED.

ART BY: NELSON DANIEL

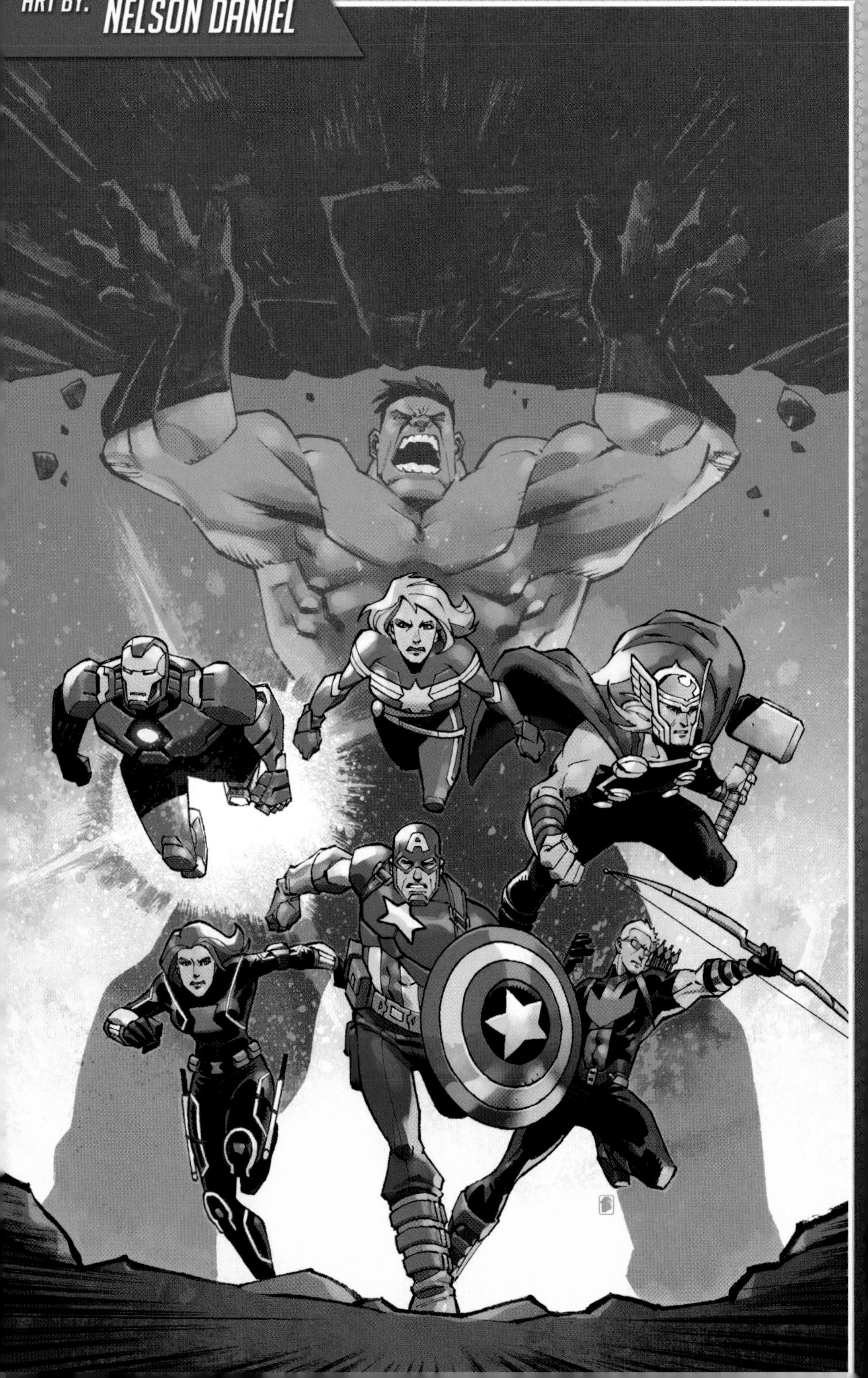

ART BY: JON SOMMARIVA

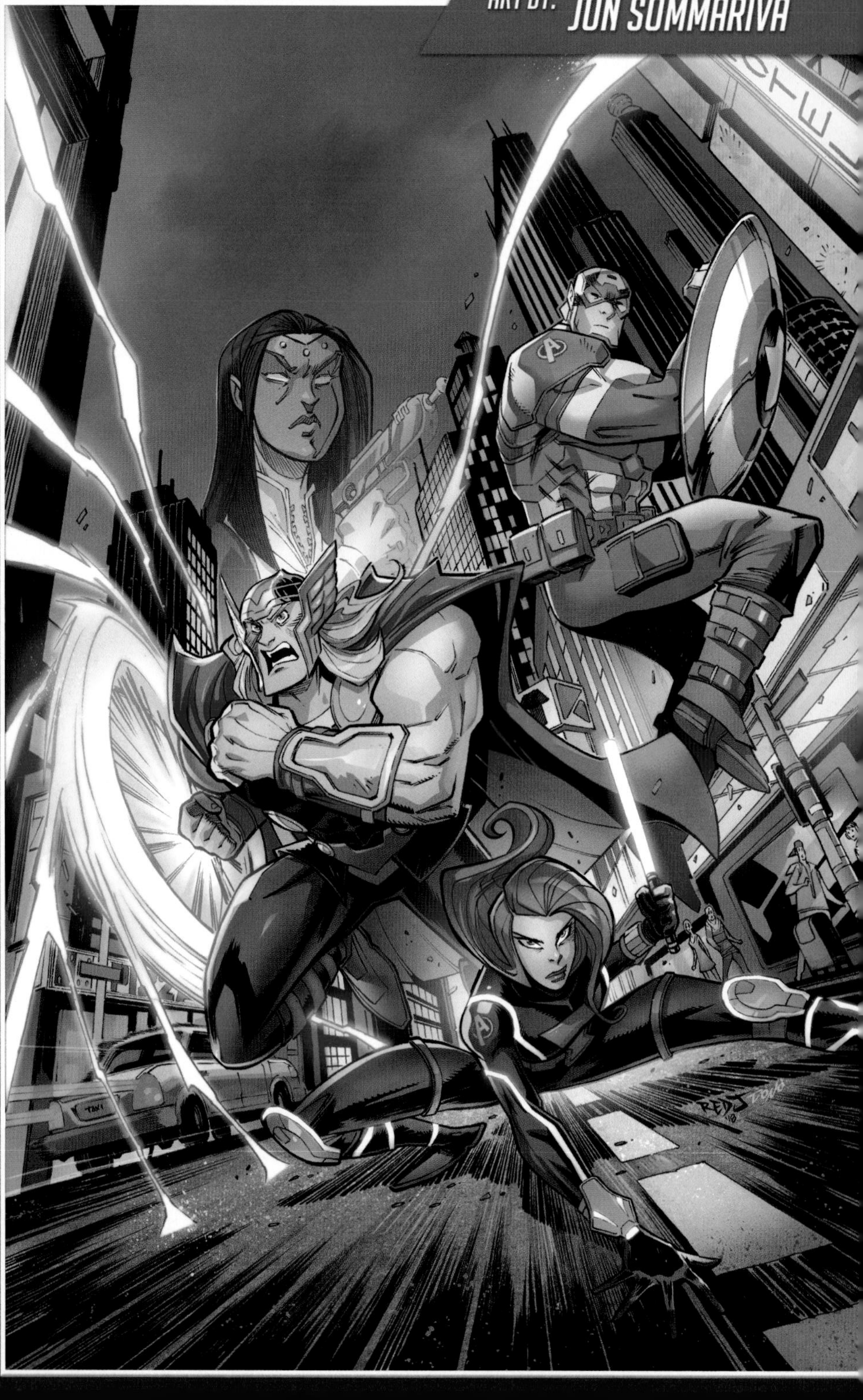

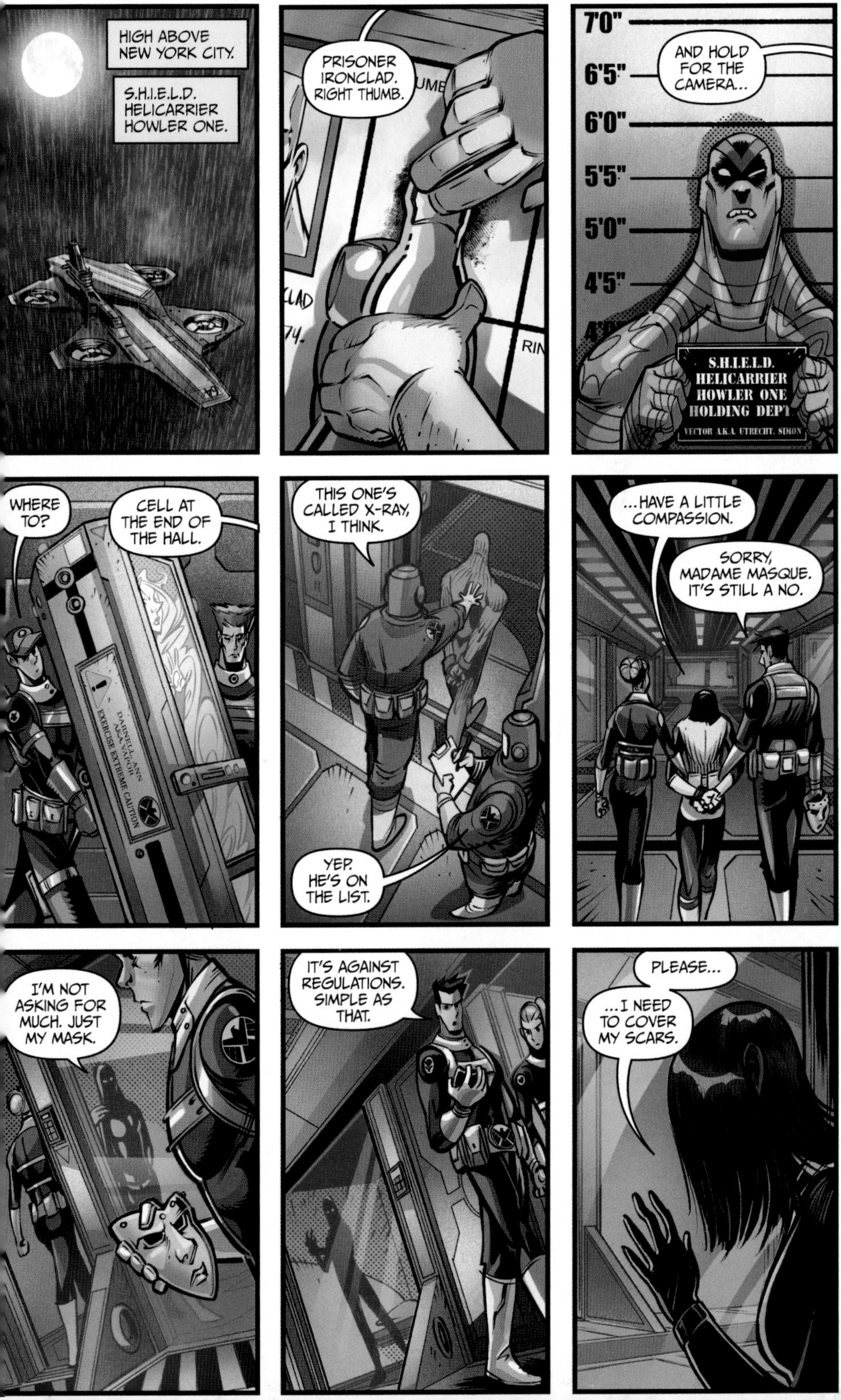
HIGH ABOVE NEW YORK CITY.
S.H.I.E.L.D. HELICARRIER HOWLER ONE.
PRISONER IRONCLAD. RIGHT THUMB.
AND HOLD FOR THE CAMERA...
S.H.I.E.L.D. HELICARRIER HOWLER ONE HOLDING DEPT.
VECTOR A.K.A. UTRECHT, SIMON
WHERE TO?
CELL AT THE END OF THE HALL.
THIS ONE'S CALLED X-RAY, I THINK.
YEP. HE'S ON THE LIST.
...HAVE A LITTLE COMPASSION.
SORRY, MADAME MASQUE. IT'S STILL A NO.
I'M NOT ASKING FOR MUCH. JUST MY MASK.
IT'S AGAINST REGULATIONS. SIMPLE AS THAT.
PLEASE...
...I NEED TO COVER MY SCARS.

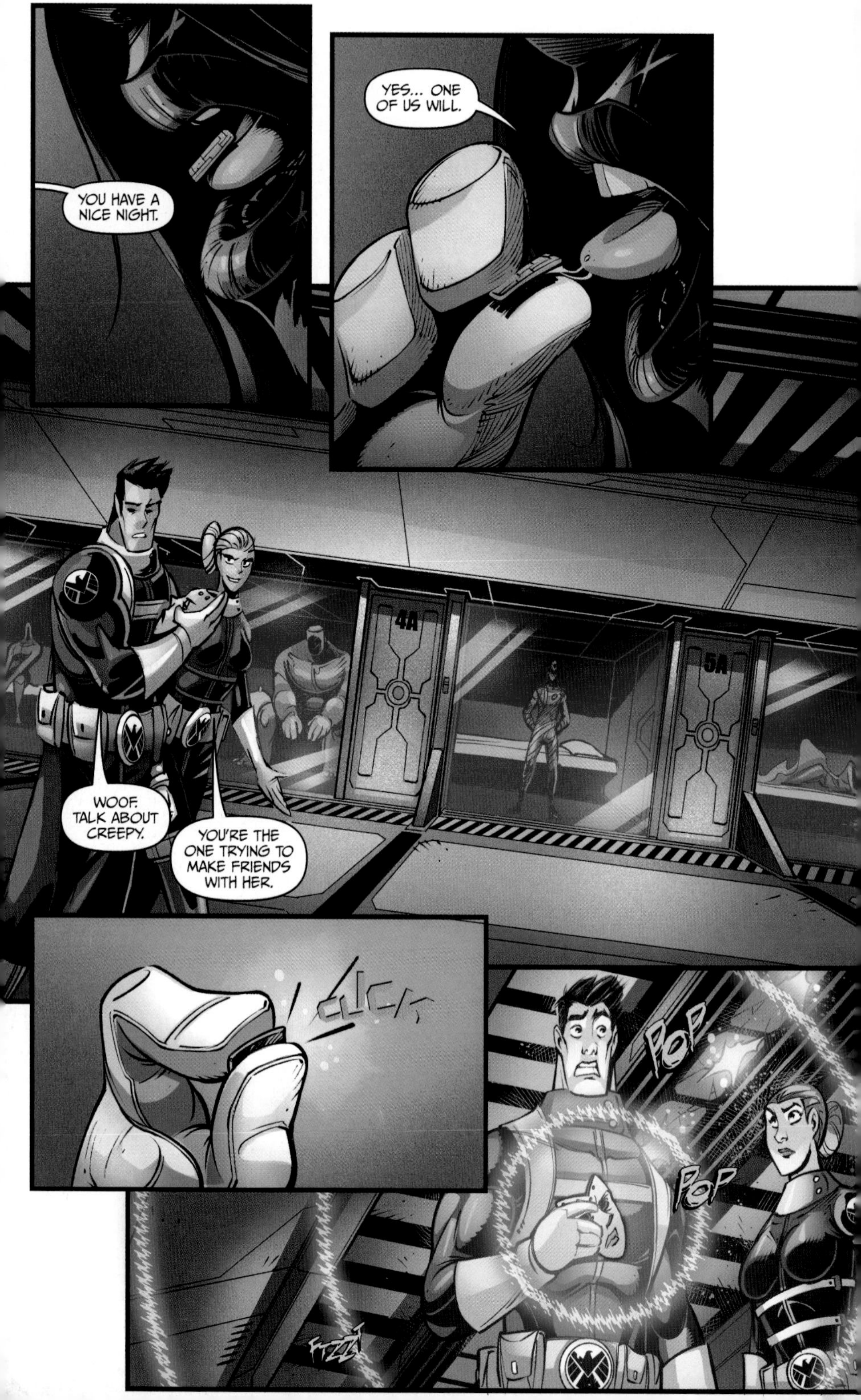
YOU HAVE A NICE NIGHT.
YES... ONE OF US WILL.
4A
5A
WOOF. TALK ABOUT CREEPY.
YOU'RE THE ONE TRYING TO MAKE FRIENDS WITH HER.
CLICK
POP
POP
FZZZT

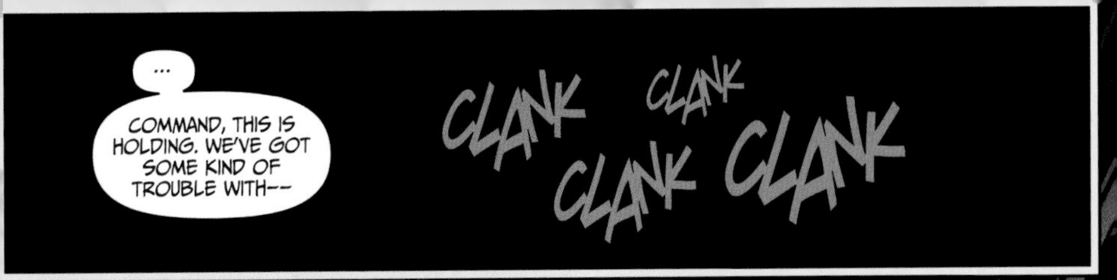
...
COMMAND, THIS IS HOLDING. WE'VE GOT SOME KIND OF TROUBLE WITH--
CLANK CLANK CLANK CLANK

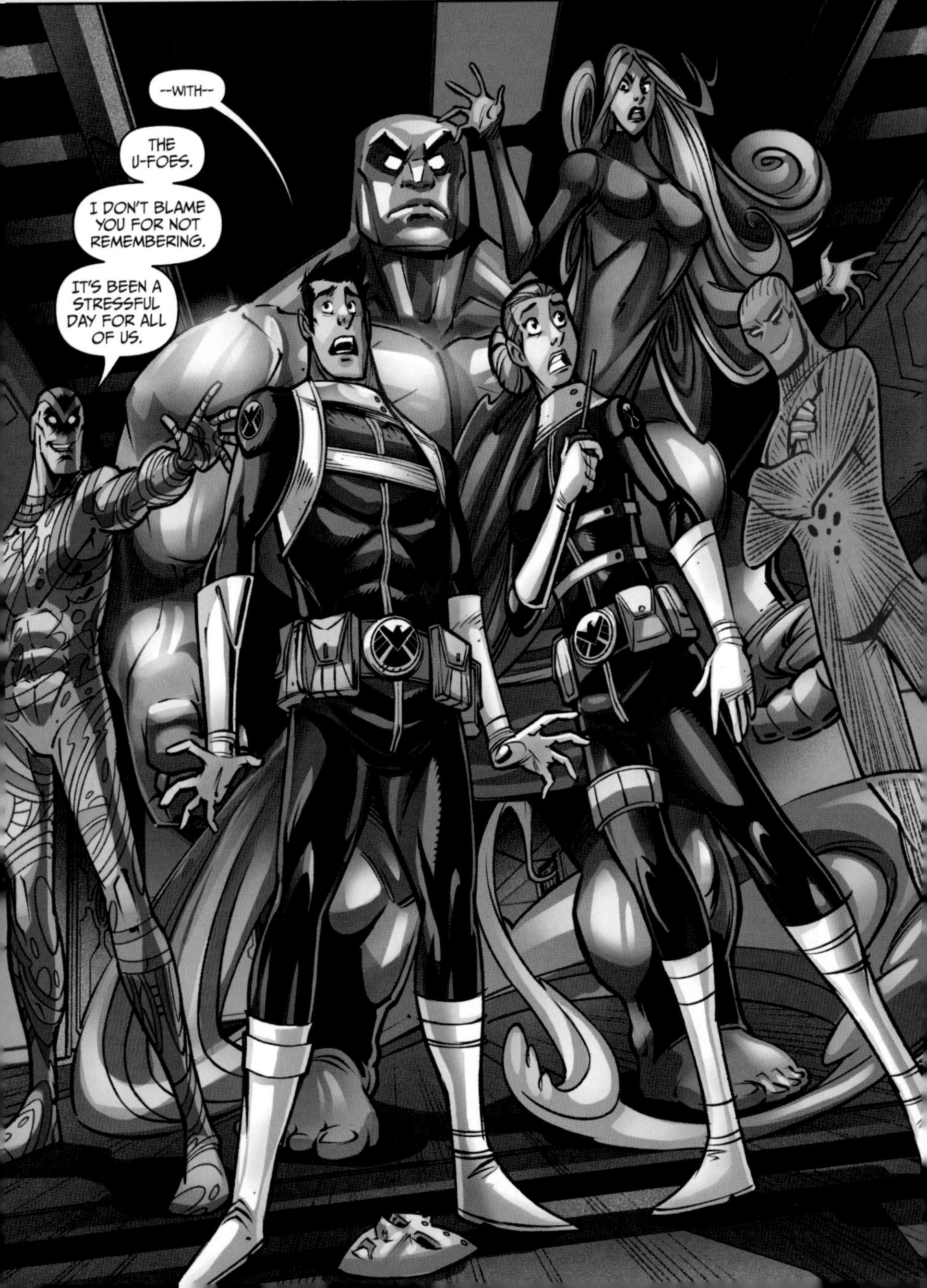
--WITH--
THE U-FOES.
I DON'T BLAME YOU FOR NOT REMEMBERING.
IT'S BEEN A STRESSFUL DAY FOR ALL OF US.

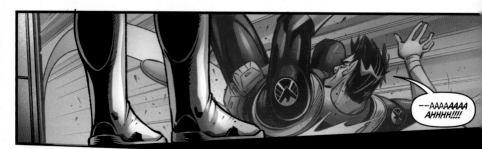

--AAAA*AAAA*AHHHH*!!!!*

NICE TRICK WITH THAT LOCALIZED EMP*.

*ELECTROMAGNETIC PULSE.

AND HERE I THOUGHT THIS THING WAS JUST FOR DRAMATIC EFFECT.

REINFORCEMENTS WILL BE HERE SOON. SO...

...ANY IDEA WHERE THEY KEEP THOSE WINGSUITS OF THEIRS?

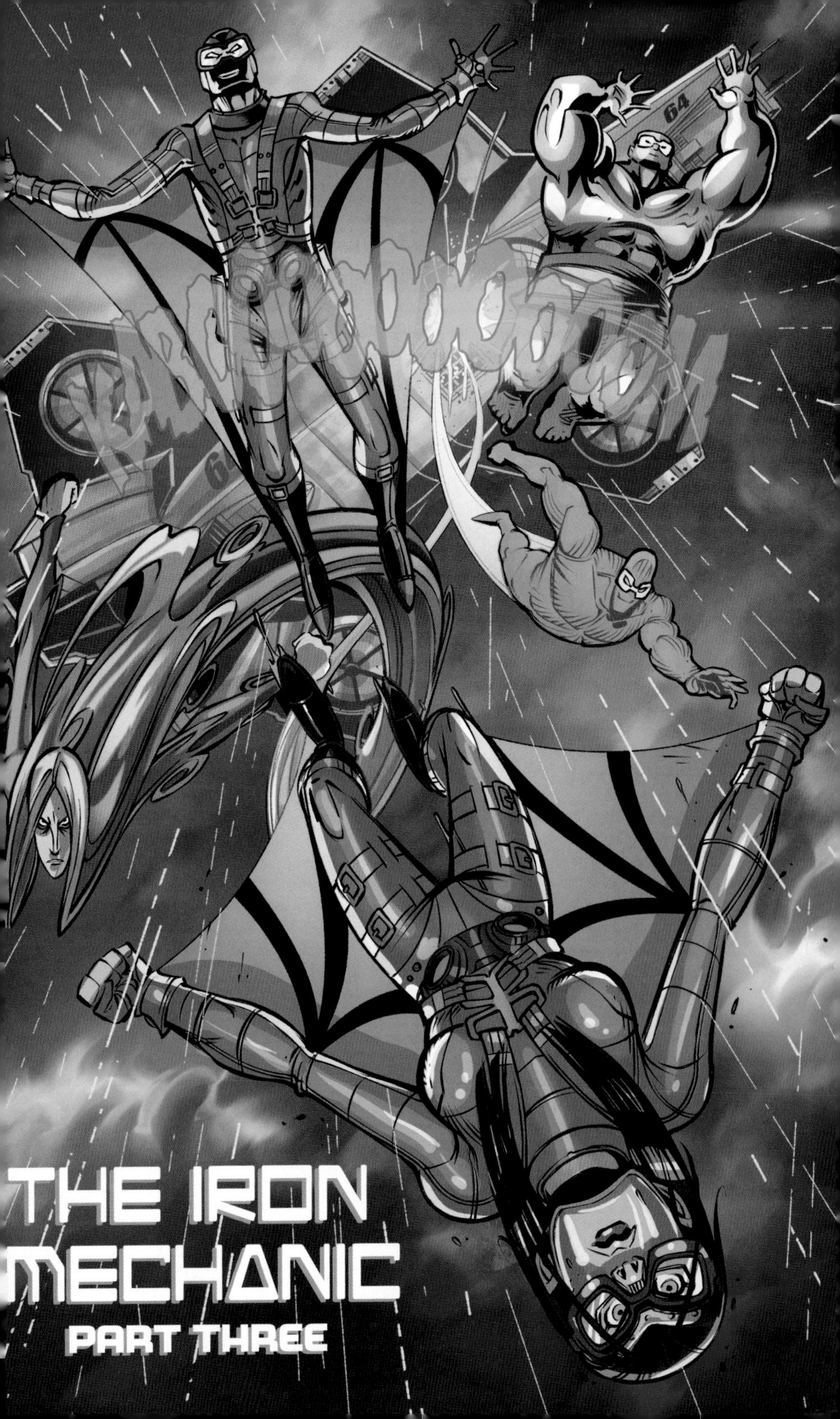
THE IRON MECHANIC
PART THREE

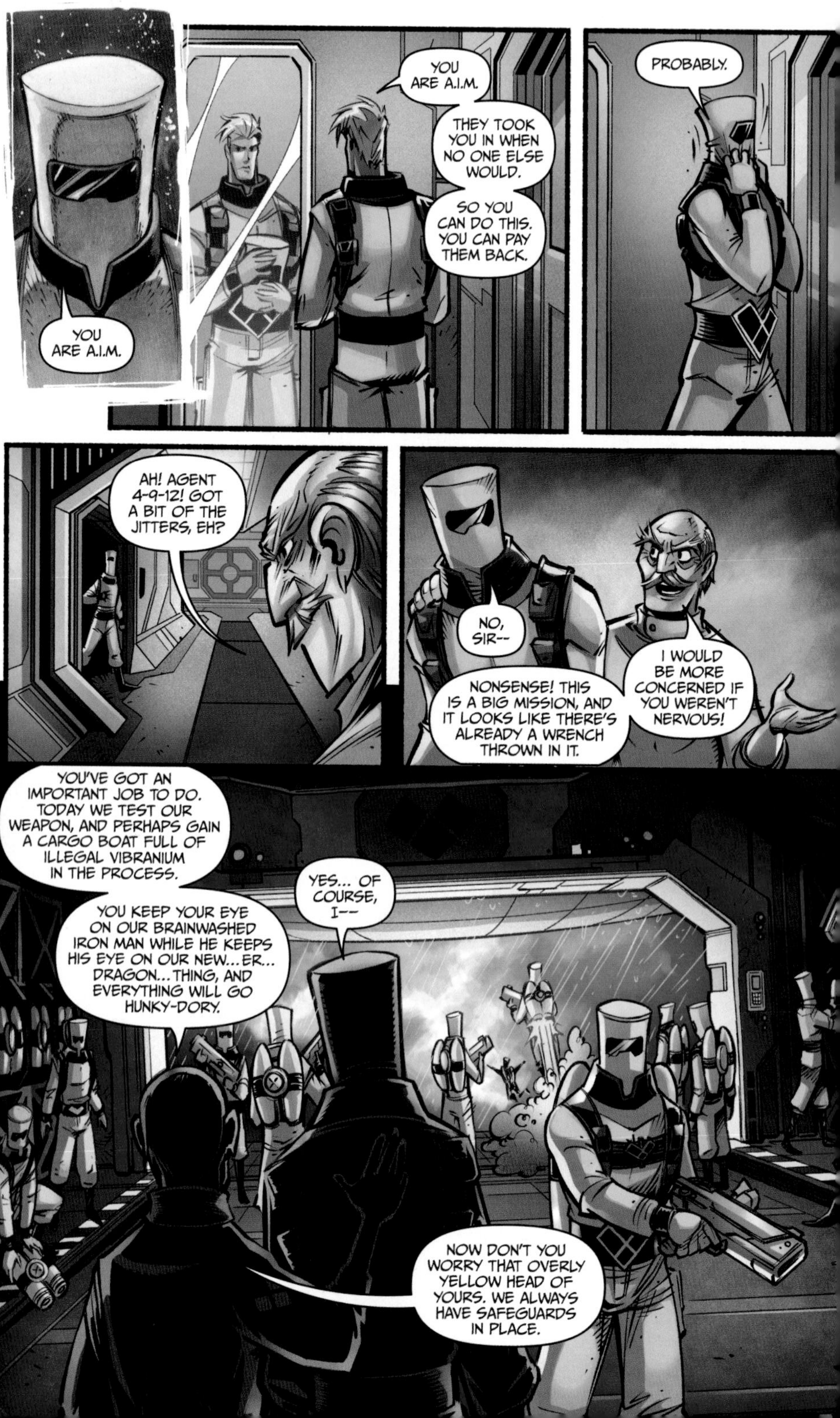
YOU ARE A.I.M.
YOU ARE A.I.M.
THEY TOOK YOU IN WHEN NO ONE ELSE WOULD.
SO YOU CAN DO THIS. YOU CAN PAY THEM BACK.
PROBABLY.
AH! AGENT 4-9-12! GOT A BIT OF THE JITTERS, EH?
NO, SIR--
I WOULD BE MORE CONCERNED IF YOU WEREN'T NERVOUS!
NONSENSE! THIS IS A BIG MISSION, AND IT LOOKS LIKE THERE'S ALREADY A WRENCH THROWN IN IT.
YOU'VE GOT AN IMPORTANT JOB TO DO. TODAY WE TEST OUR WEAPON, AND PERHAPS GAIN A CARGO BOAT FULL OF ILLEGAL VIBRANIUM IN THE PROCESS.
YOU KEEP YOUR EYE ON OUR BRAINWASHED IRON MAN WHILE HE KEEPS HIS EYE ON OUR NEW...ER... DRAGON...THING, AND EVERYTHING WILL GO HUNKY-DORY.
YES... OF COURSE, I--
NOW DON'T YOU WORRY THAT OVERLY YELLOW HEAD OF YOURS. WE ALWAYS HAVE SAFEGUARDS IN PLACE.

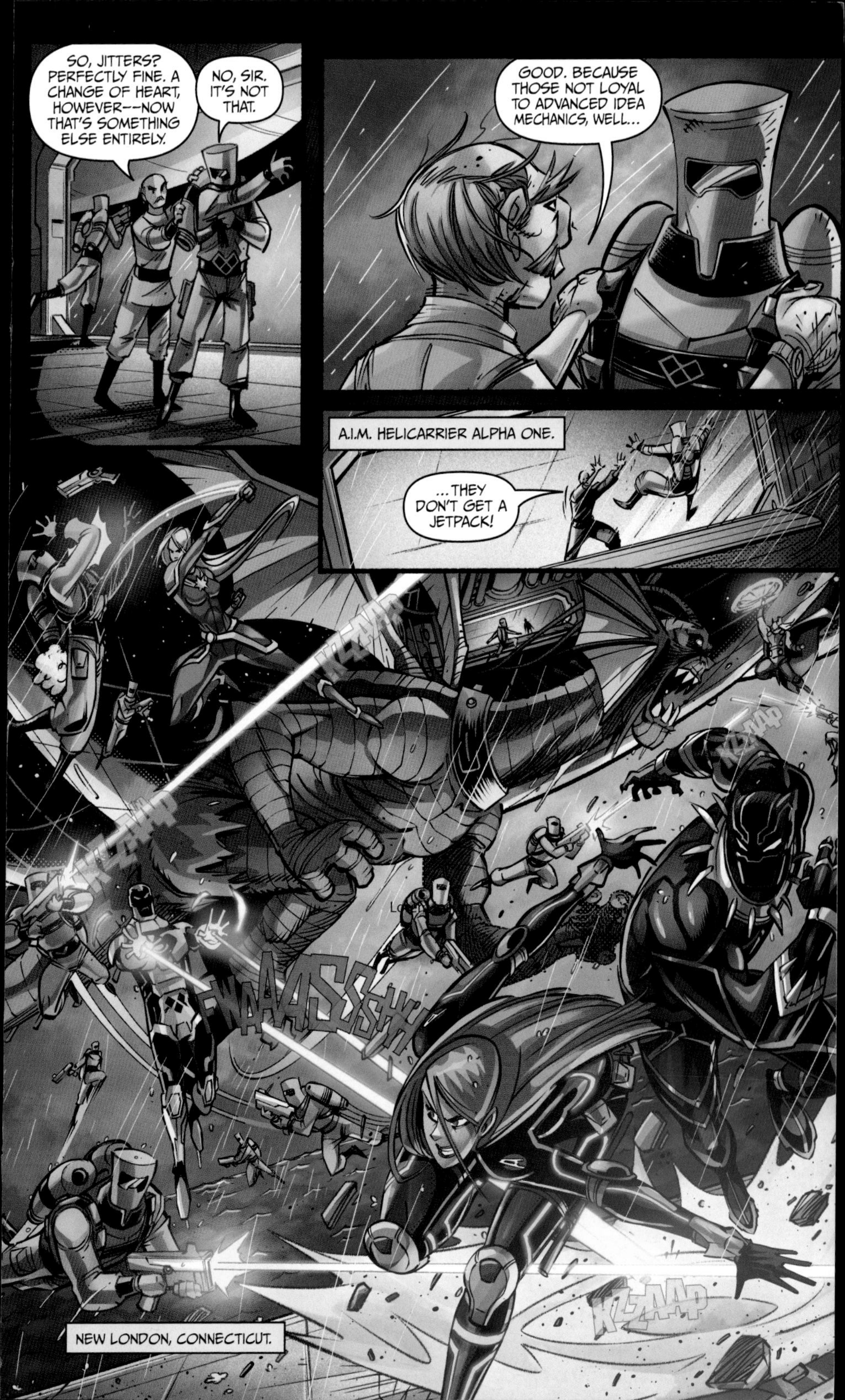
SO, JITTERS? PERFECTLY FINE. A CHANGE OF HEART, HOWEVER--NOW THAT'S SOMETHING ELSE ENTIRELY.
NO, SIR. IT'S NOT THAT.
GOOD. BECAUSE THOSE NOT LOYAL TO ADVANCED IDEA MECHANICS, WELL...
A.I.M. HELICARRIER ALPHA ONE.
...THEY DON'T GET A JETPACK!
FWAAASSSHK
KZAAP
NEW LONDON, CONNECTICUT.

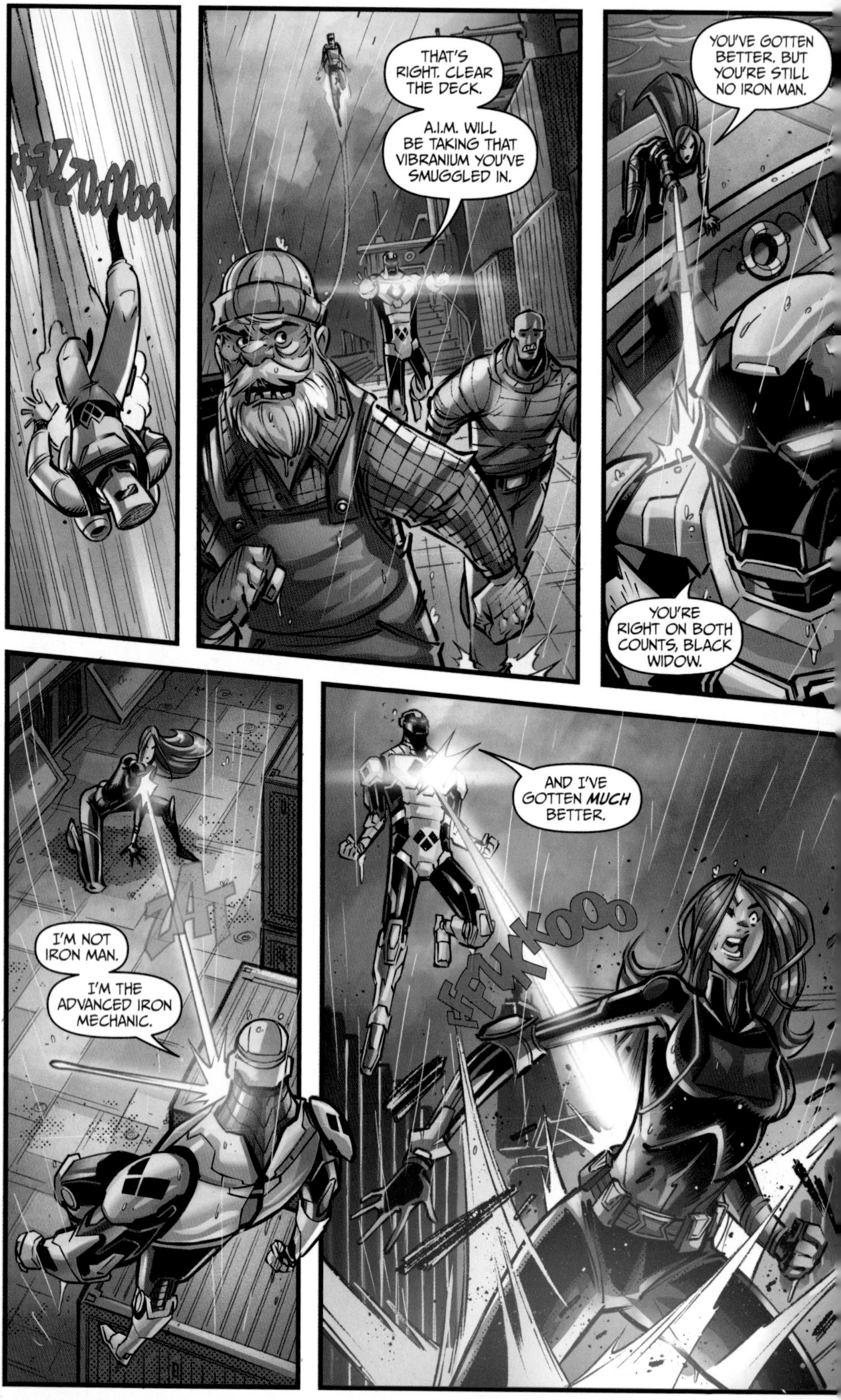
FZZZOOOOOM
THAT'S RIGHT. CLEAR THE DECK.
A.I.M. WILL BE TAKING THAT VIBRANIUM YOU'VE SMUGGLED IN.
YOU'VE GOTTEN BETTER. BUT YOU'RE STILL NO IRON MAN.
ZAT
YOU'RE RIGHT ON BOTH COUNTS, BLACK WIDOW.
ZAT
I'M NOT IRON MAN.
I'M THE ADVANCED IRON MECHANIC.
AND I'VE GOTTEN *MUCH* BETTER.
FFAKOOO

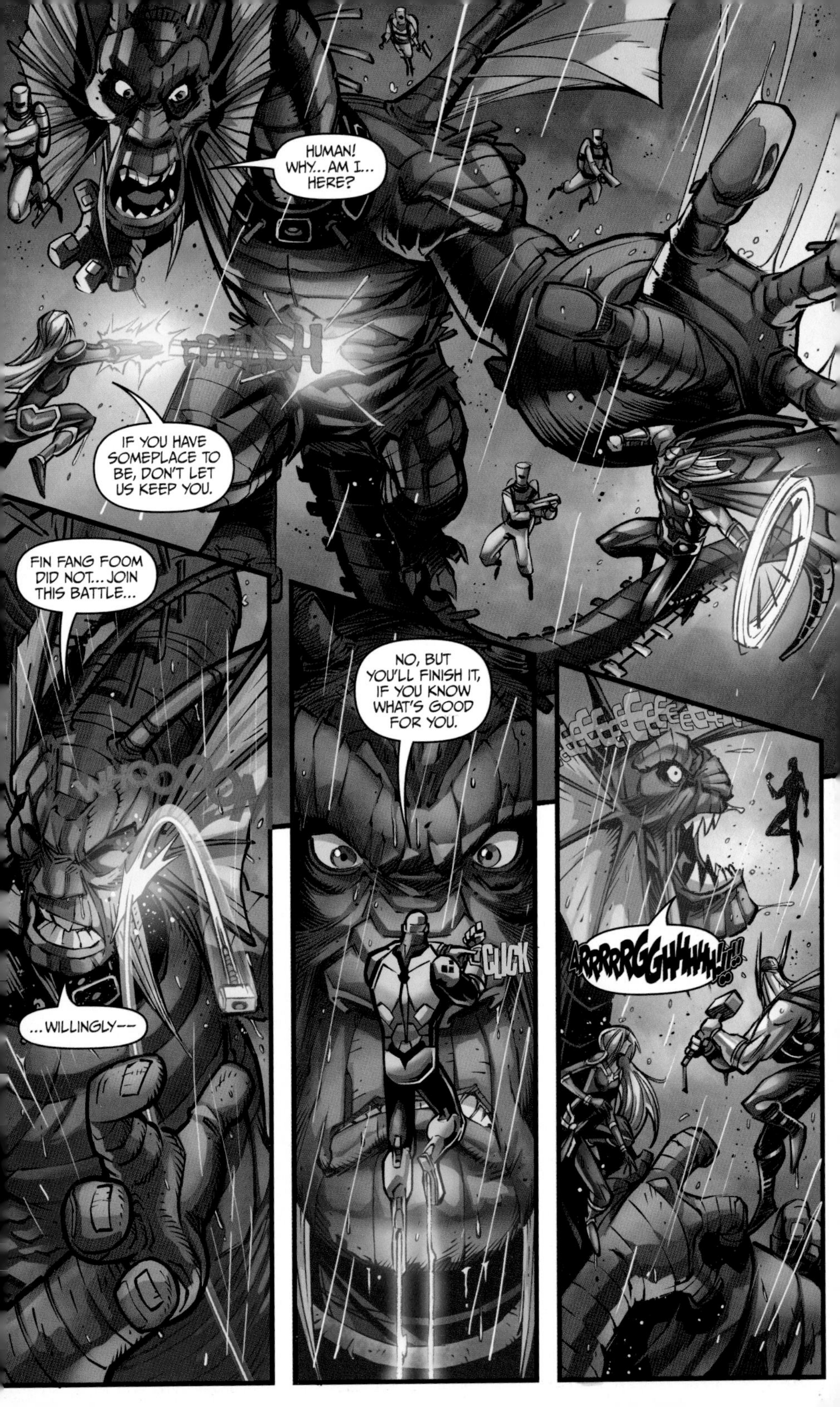
HUMAN! WHY...AM I... HERE?
FTAASH
IF YOU HAVE SOMEPLACE TO BE, DON'T LET US KEEP YOU.
FIN FANG FOOM DID NOT...JOIN THIS BATTLE...
...WILLINGLY--
NO, BUT YOU'LL FINISH IT, IF YOU KNOW WHAT'S GOOD FOR YOU.
CLICK
ARRRRRGGHHHHH!!!

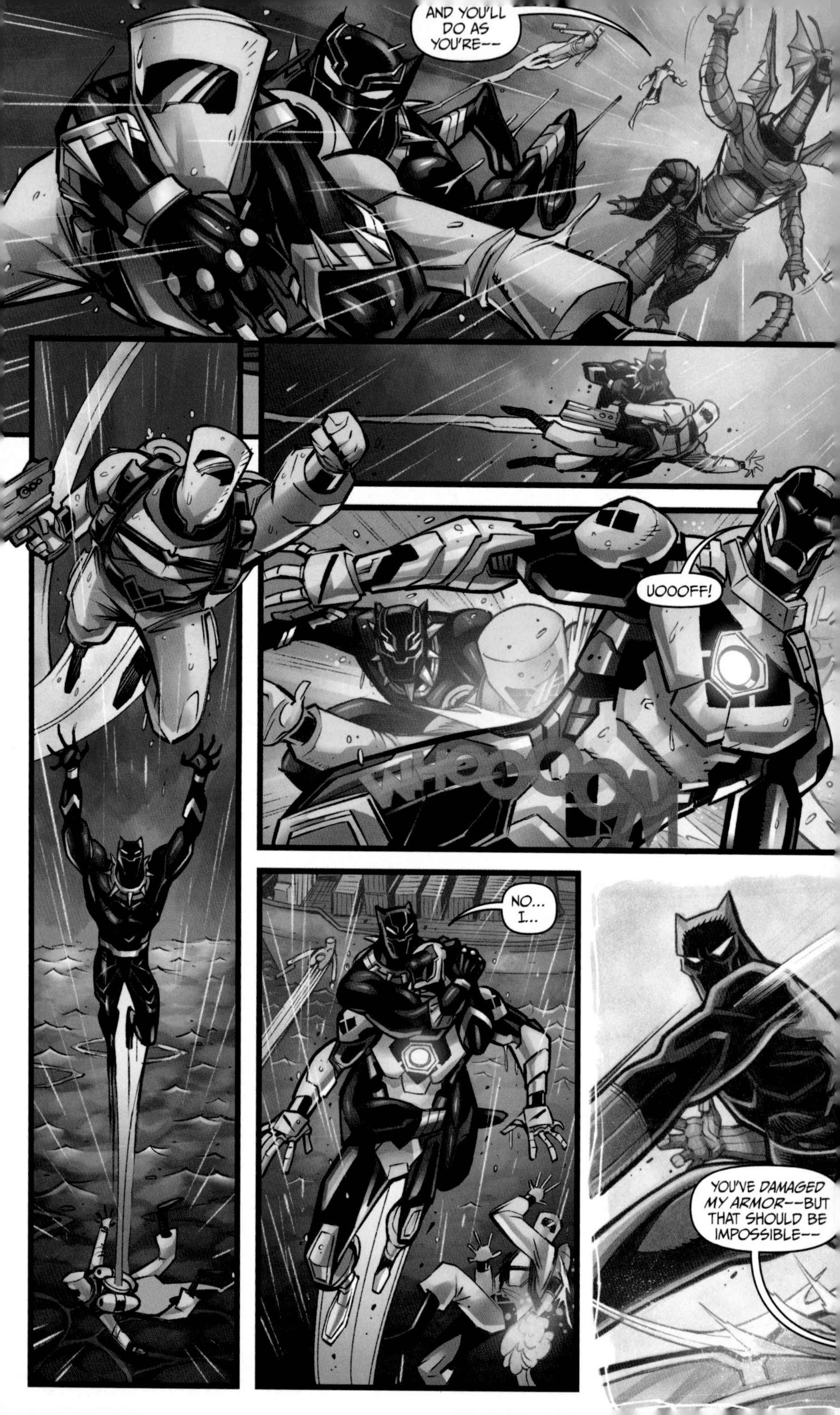
AND YOU'LL DO AS YOU'RE--
UOOOFF!
WHOOOOM
NO... I...
YOU'VE *DAMAGED* MY *ARMOR*--BUT THAT SHOULD BE IMPOSSIBLE--

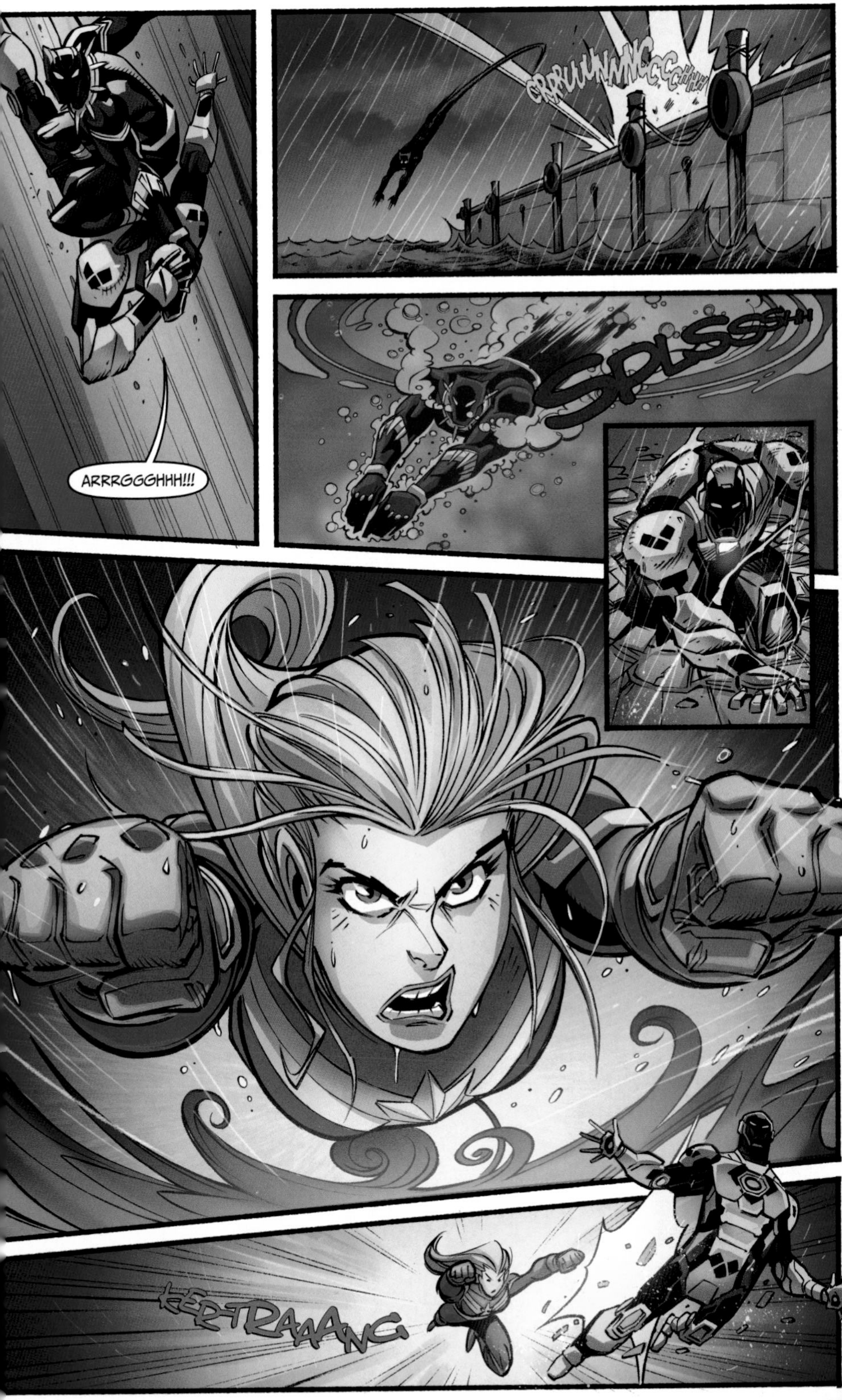
ARRRGGGHHH!!!
CRRUUUNNNGGCHHH
SPLSSSSHH
KERTRAAANG

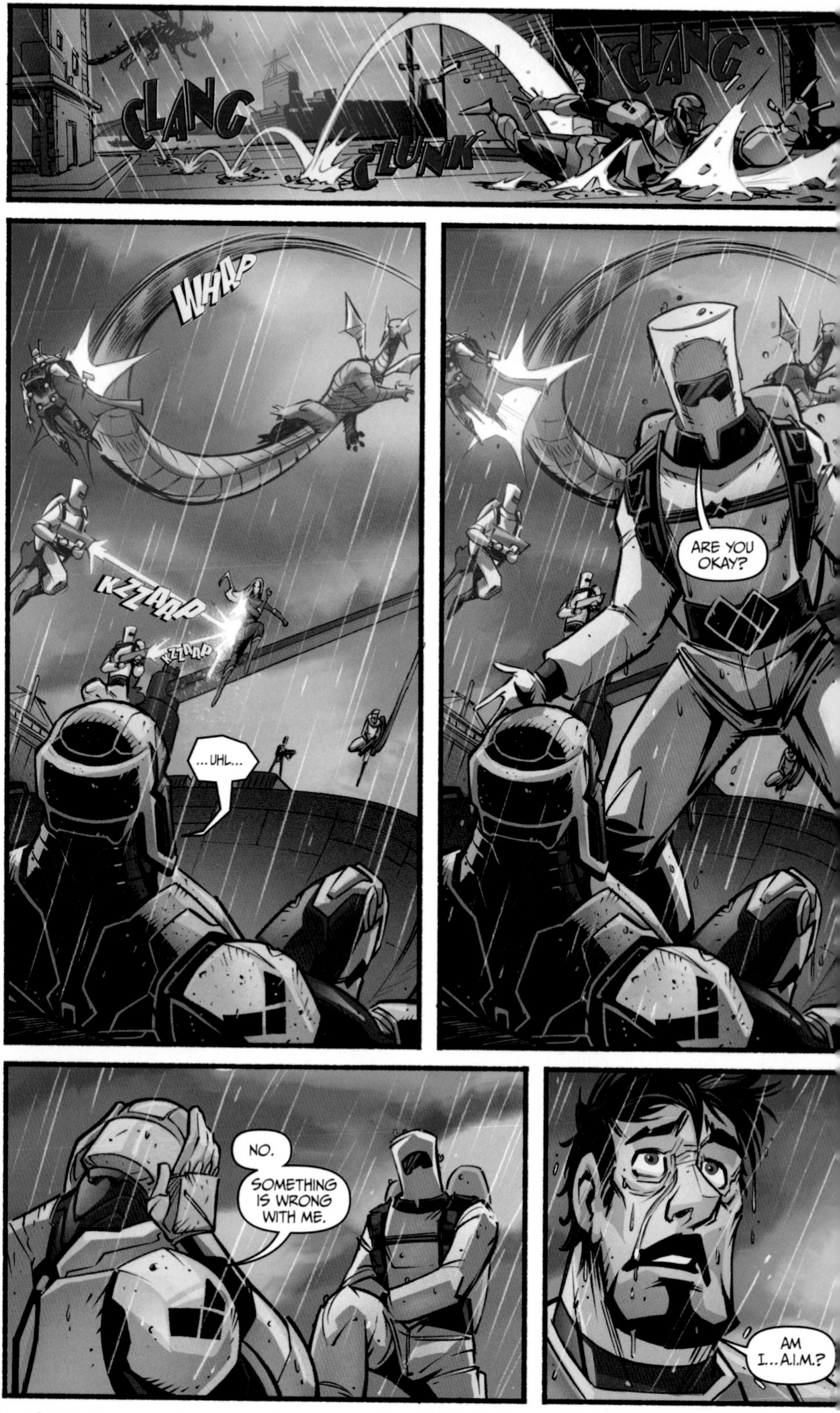
CLANG
CLUNK
CLANG
WHAP
KZZAARP
KZZAARP
...UHL...
ARE YOU OKAY?
NO.
SOMETHING IS WRONG WITH ME.
AM I...A.I.M.?

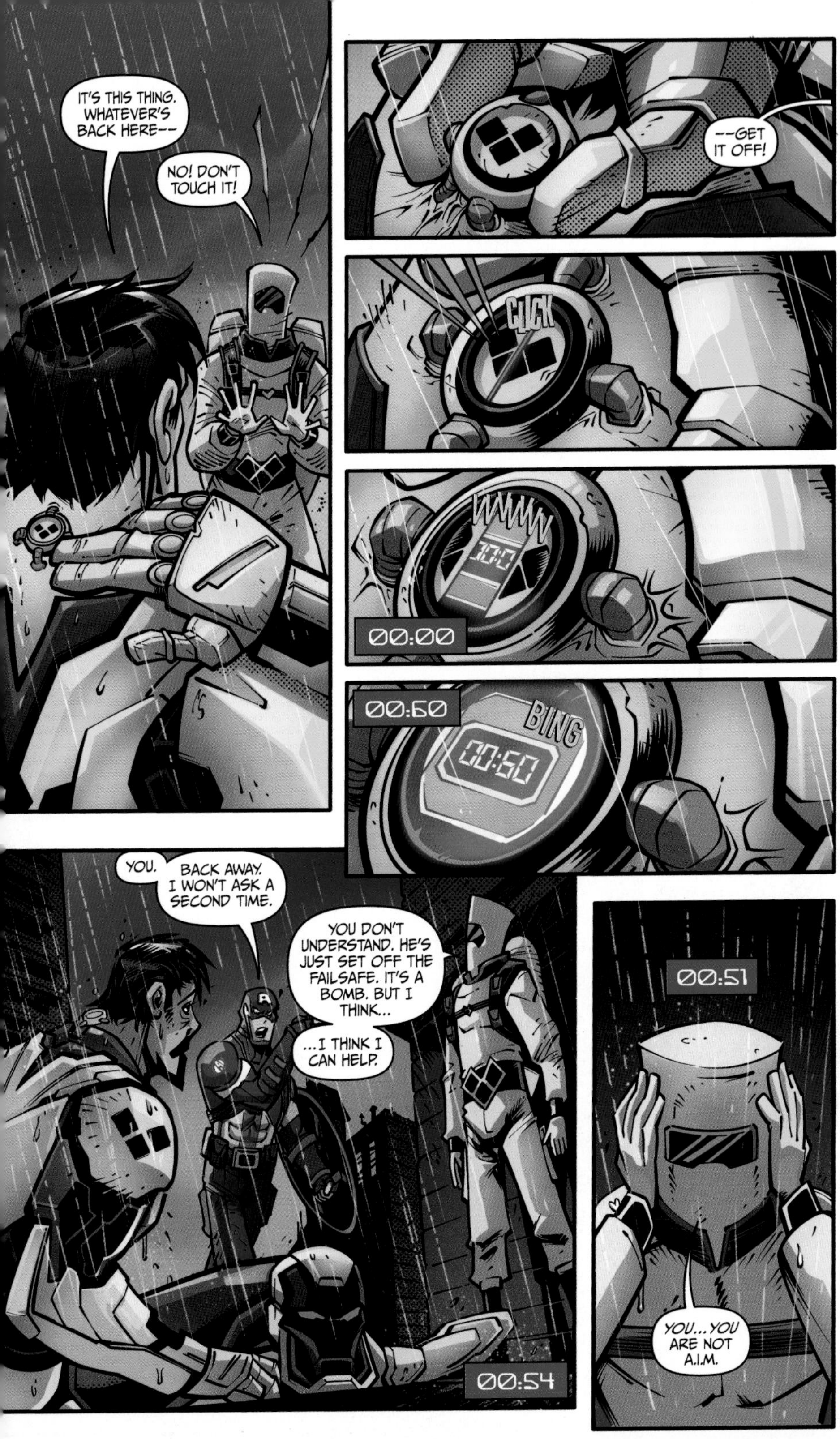

IT'S THIS THING. WHATEVER'S BACK HERE--
NO! DON'T TOUCH IT!
--GET IT OFF!
CLICK
WWWWW
00:00
00:60
BING
00:60
YOU.
BACK AWAY. I WON'T ASK A SECOND TIME.
YOU DON'T UNDERSTAND. HE'S JUST SET OFF THE FAILSAFE. IT'S A BOMB. BUT I THINK...
...I THINK I CAN HELP.
00:54
00:51
YOU...YOU ARE NOT A.I.M.

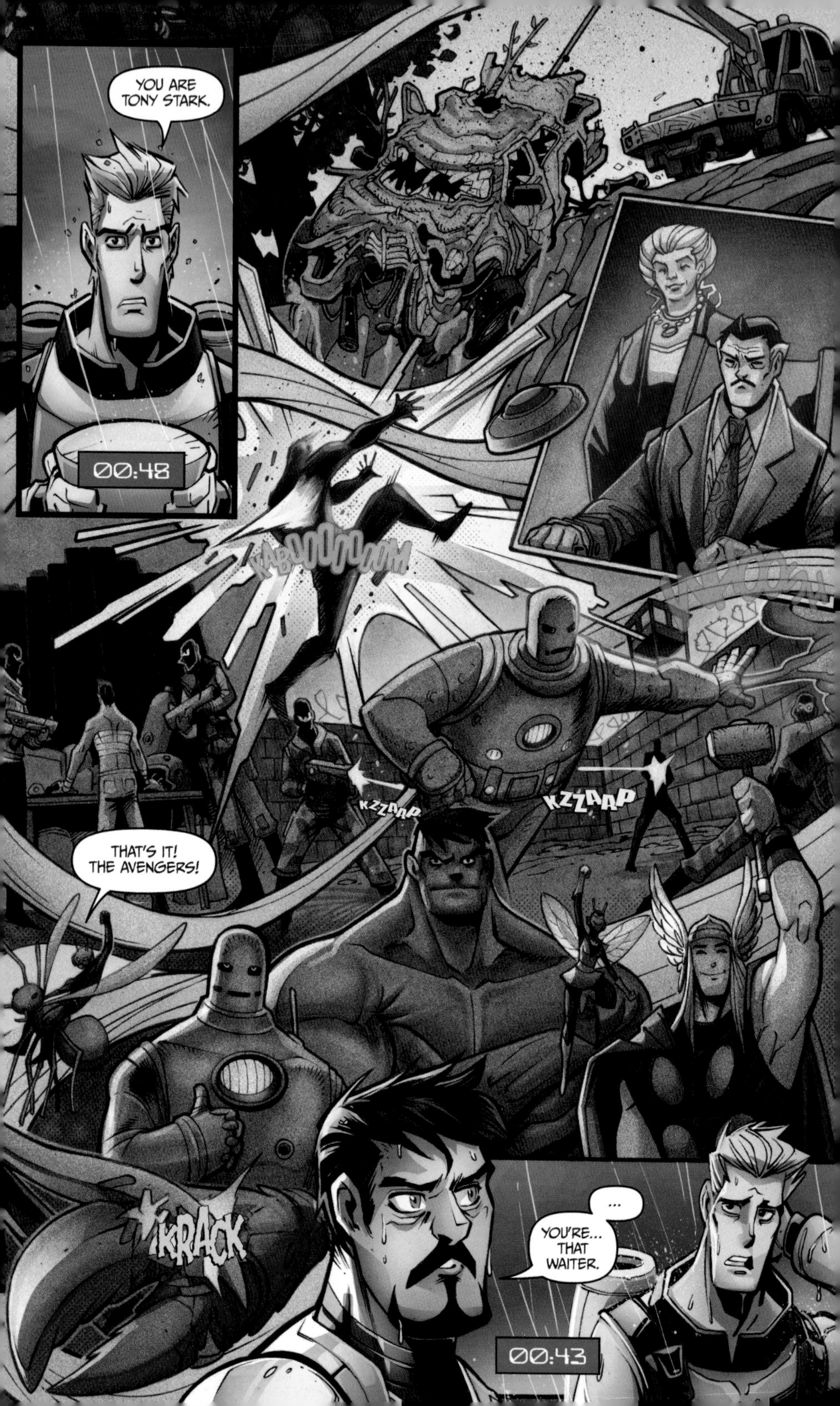
YOU ARE TONY STARK.
00:48
KABOOOOOOOM
KZZAAP
KZZAAP
THAT'S IT! THE AVENGERS!
KRACK
...
YOU'RE... THAT WAITER.
00:43

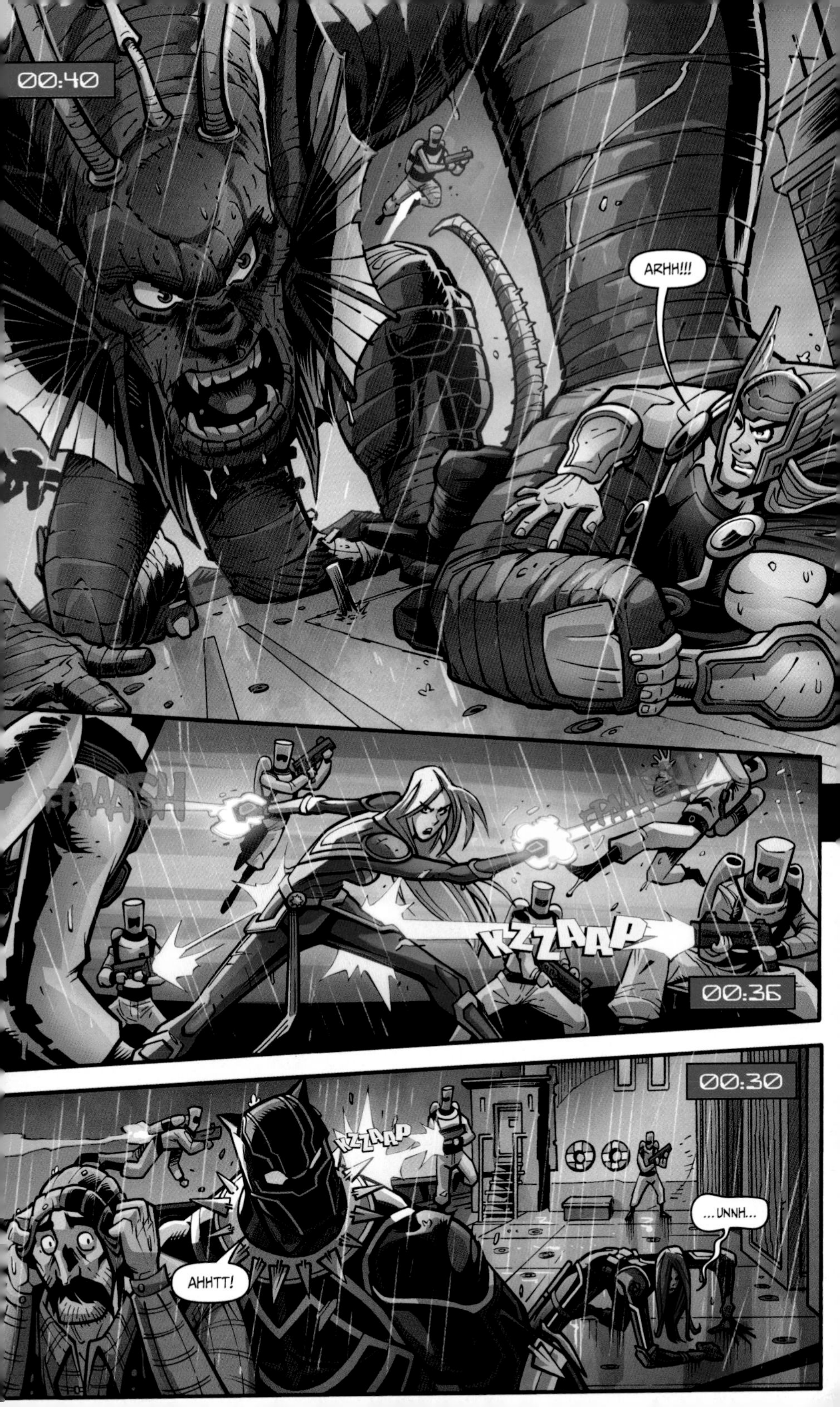
00:40
ARHH!!!
FRAAASH
FRAAASH
KZZAAP
00:36
00:30
KZZAAP
...UNNH...
AHHTT!

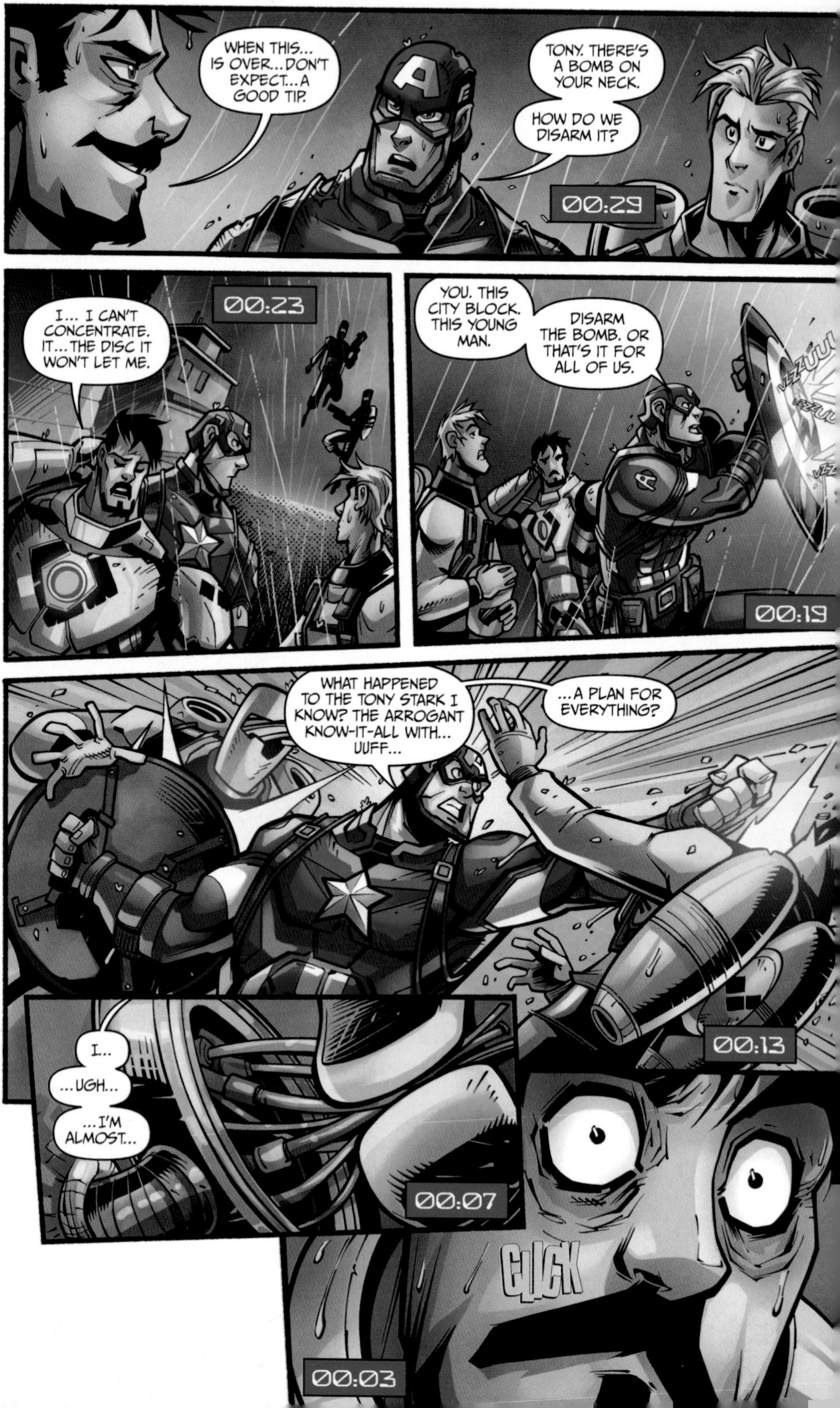
WHEN THIS... IS OVER...DON'T EXPECT...A GOOD TIP.
TONY. THERE'S A BOMB ON YOUR NECK.
HOW DO WE DISARM IT?
00:29
00:23
I... I CAN'T CONCENTRATE. IT...THE DISC IT WON'T LET ME.
YOU. THIS CITY BLOCK. THIS YOUNG MAN.
DISARM THE BOMB. OR THAT'S IT FOR ALL OF US.
VZZZUU
00:19
WHAT HAPPENED TO THE TONY STARK I KNOW? THE ARROGANT KNOW-IT-ALL WITH... UUFF...
...A PLAN FOR EVERYTHING?
00:13
I...
...UGH...
...I'M ALMOST...
00:07
CLICK
00:03

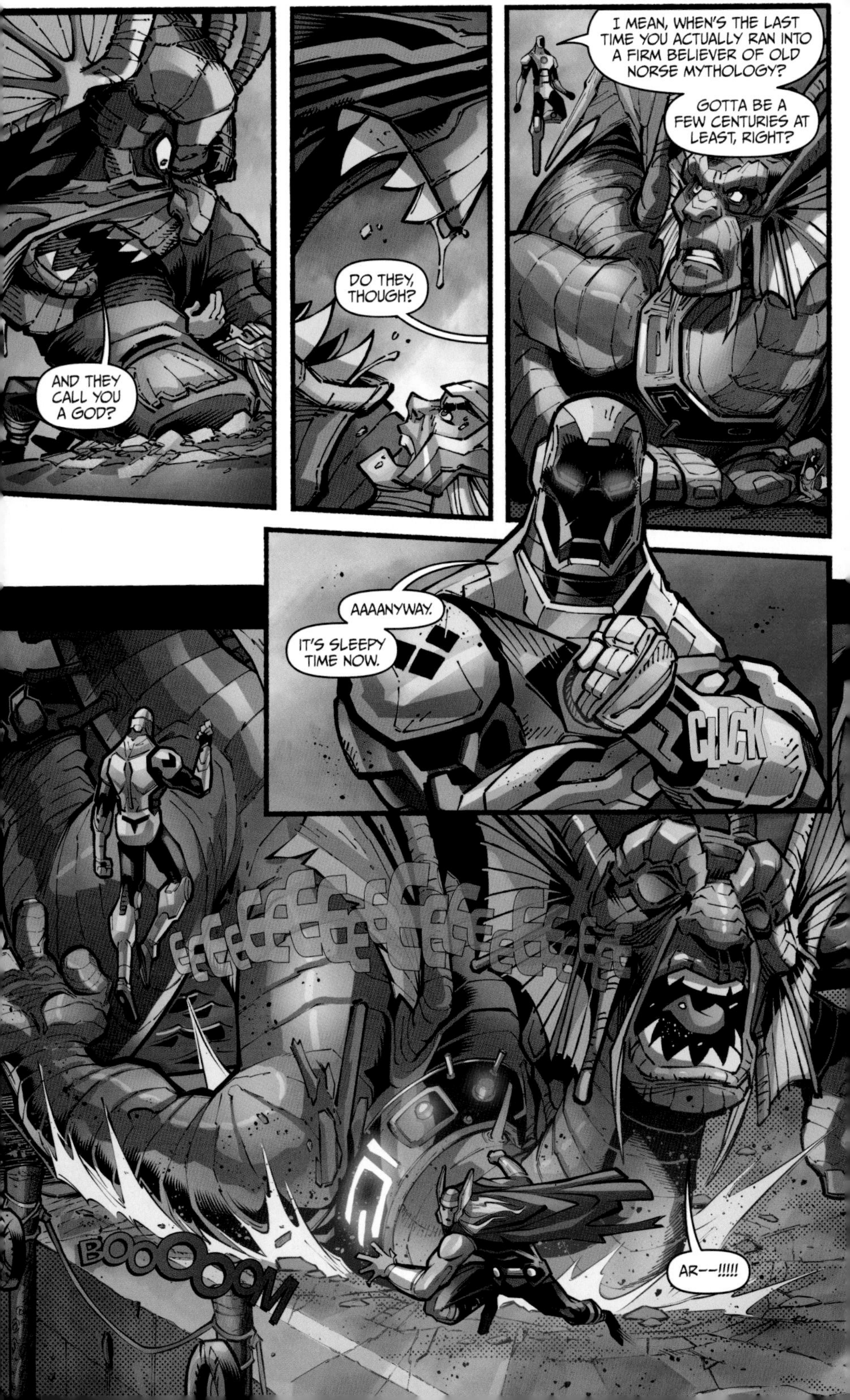
AND THEY CALL YOU A GOD?
DO THEY, THOUGH?
I MEAN, WHEN'S THE LAST TIME YOU ACTUALLY RAN INTO A FIRM BELIEVER OF OLD NORSE MYTHOLOGY?
GOTTA BE A FEW CENTURIES AT LEAST, RIGHT?
AAAANYWAY.
IT'S SLEEPY TIME NOW.
CLICK
EEEEEEEEEEEEEEEEEEEEEE
BOOOOOM
AR--!!!!!

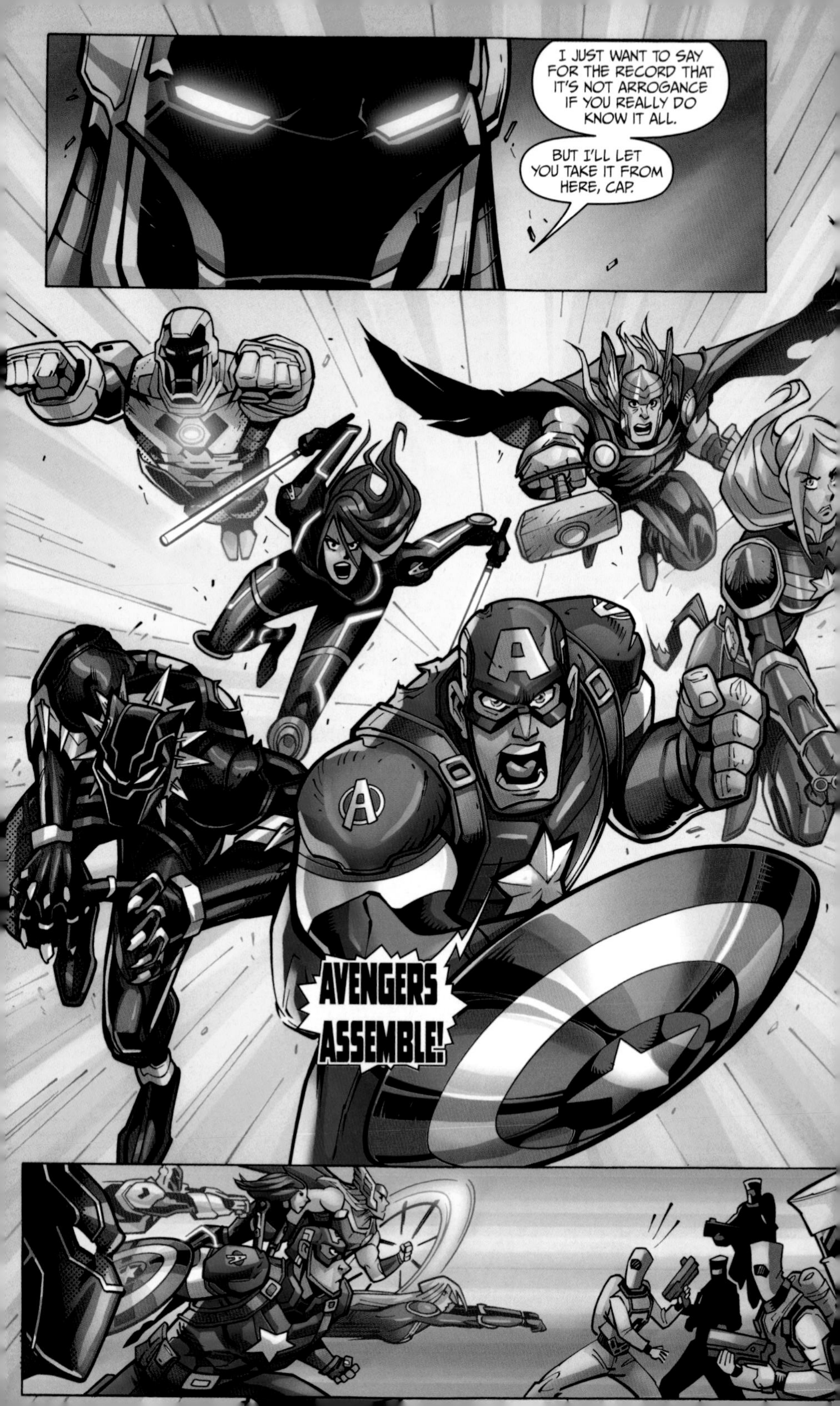
I JUST WANT TO SAY FOR THE RECORD THAT IT'S NOT ARROGANCE IF YOU REALLY DO KNOW IT ALL.
BUT I'LL LET YOU TAKE IT FROM HERE, CAP.
AVENGERS ASSEMBLE!

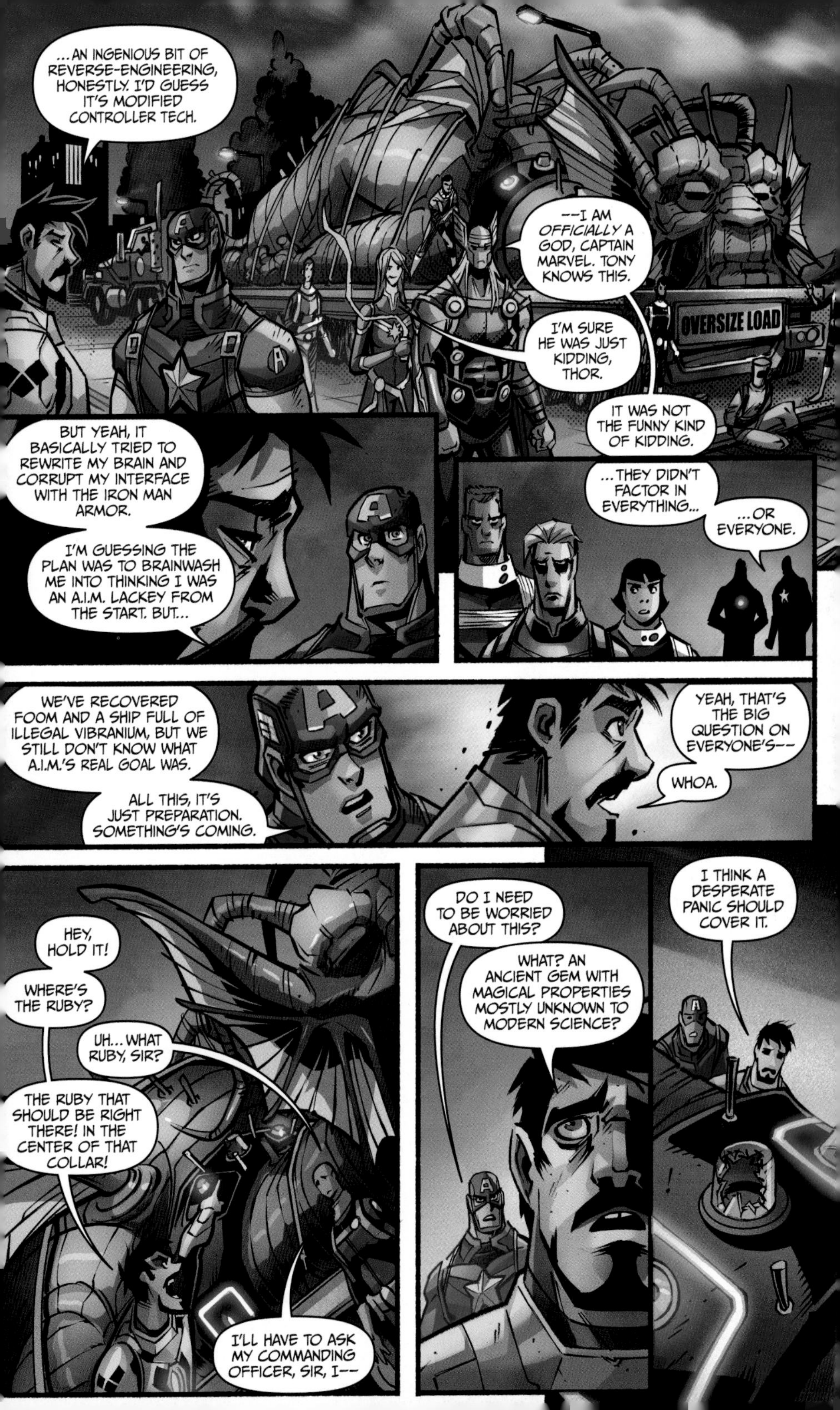

...AN INGENIOUS BIT OF REVERSE-ENGINEERING, HONESTLY. I'D GUESS IT'S MODIFIED CONTROLLER TECH.
--I AM *OFFICIALLY* A GOD, CAPTAIN MARVEL. TONY KNOWS THIS.
OVERSIZE LOAD
I'M SURE HE WAS JUST KIDDING, THOR.
IT WAS NOT THE FUNNY KIND OF KIDDING.
BUT YEAH, IT BASICALLY TRIED TO REWRITE MY BRAIN AND CORRUPT MY INTERFACE WITH THE IRON MAN ARMOR.
I'M GUESSING THE PLAN WAS TO BRAINWASH ME INTO THINKING I WAS AN A.I.M. LACKEY FROM THE START. BUT...
...THEY DIDN'T FACTOR IN EVERYTHING...
...OR EVERYONE.
WE'VE RECOVERED FOOM AND A SHIP FULL OF ILLEGAL VIBRANIUM, BUT WE STILL DON'T KNOW WHAT A.I.M.'S REAL GOAL WAS.
ALL THIS, IT'S JUST PREPARATION. SOMETHING'S COMING.
YEAH, THAT'S THE BIG QUESTION ON EVERYONE'S--
WHOA.
HEY, HOLD IT!
WHERE'S THE RUBY?
UH...WHAT RUBY, SIR?
THE RUBY THAT SHOULD BE RIGHT THERE! IN THE CENTER OF THAT COLLAR!
I'LL HAVE TO ASK MY COMMANDING OFFICER, SIR, I--
DO I NEED TO BE WORRIED ABOUT THIS?
WHAT? AN ANCIENT GEM WITH MAGICAL PROPERTIES MOSTLY UNKNOWN TO MODERN SCIENCE?
I THINK A DESPERATE PANIC SHOULD COVER IT.

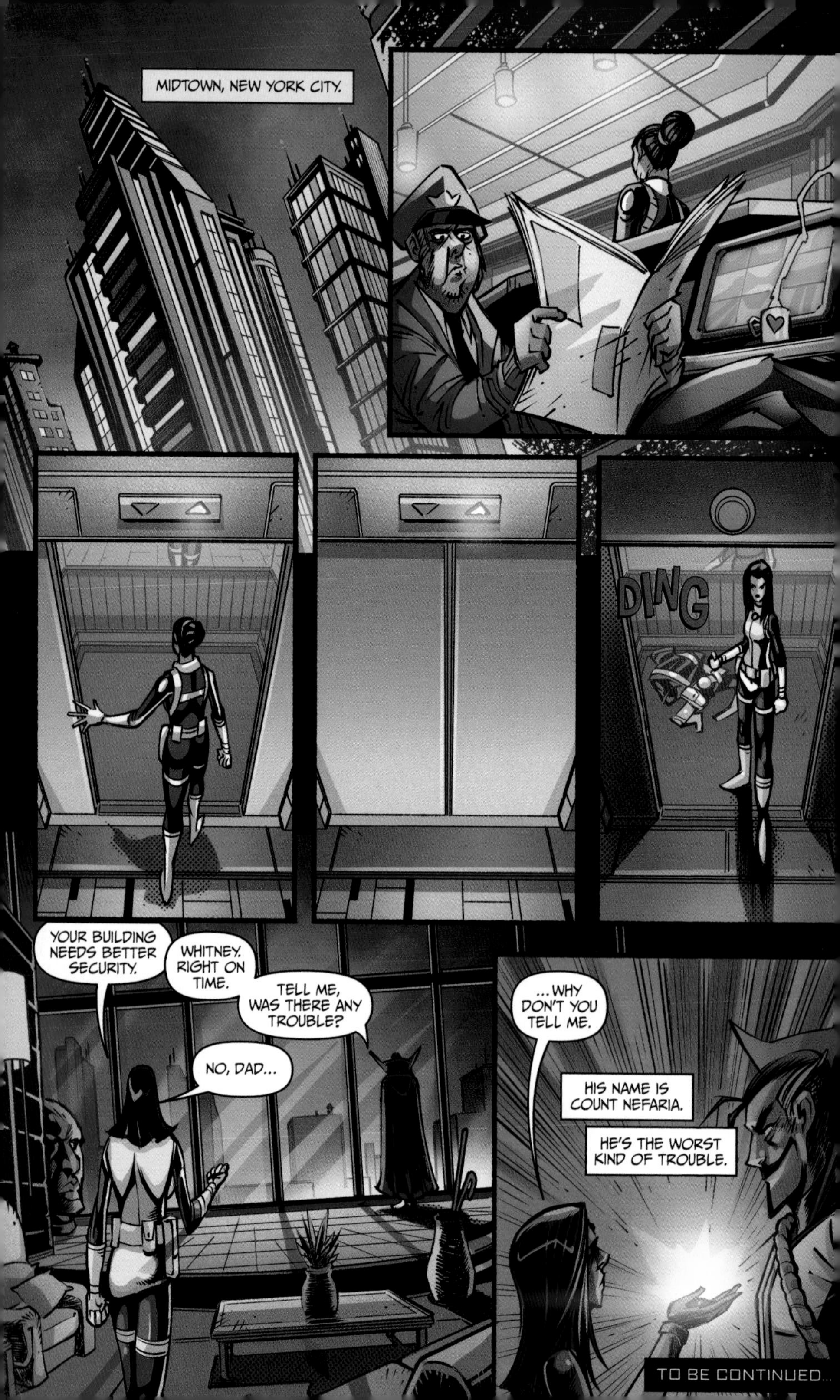
MIDTOWN, NEW YORK CITY.
DING
YOUR BUILDING NEEDS BETTER SECURITY.
WHITNEY. RIGHT ON TIME.
TELL ME, WAS THERE ANY TROUBLE?
NO, DAD...
...WHY DON'T YOU TELL ME.
HIS NAME IS COUNT NEFARIA.
HE'S THE WORST KIND OF TROUBLE.
TO BE CONTINUED...

ART BY: RYAN JAMPOLE

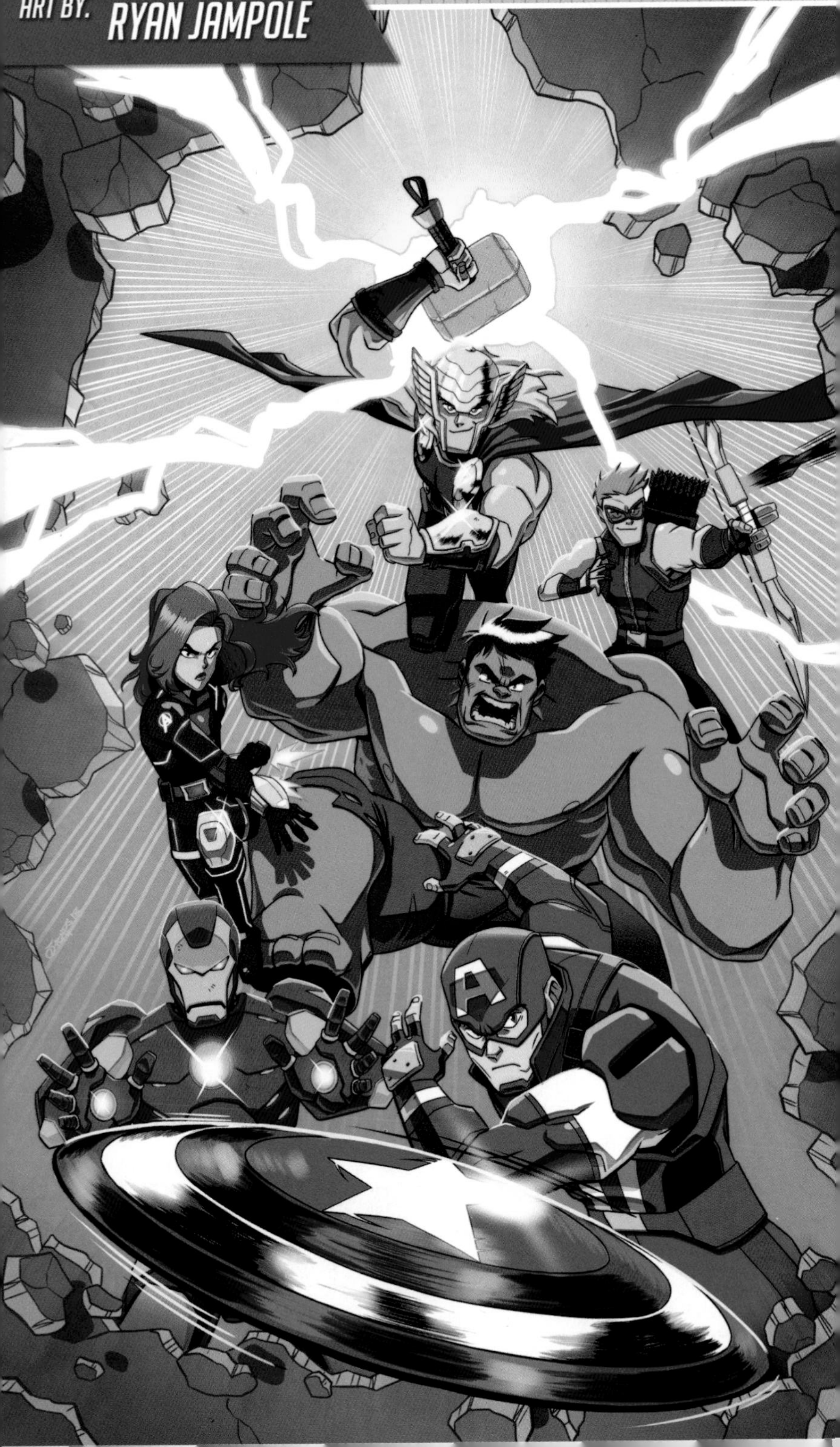

ART BY: SOPHIE CAMPBELL

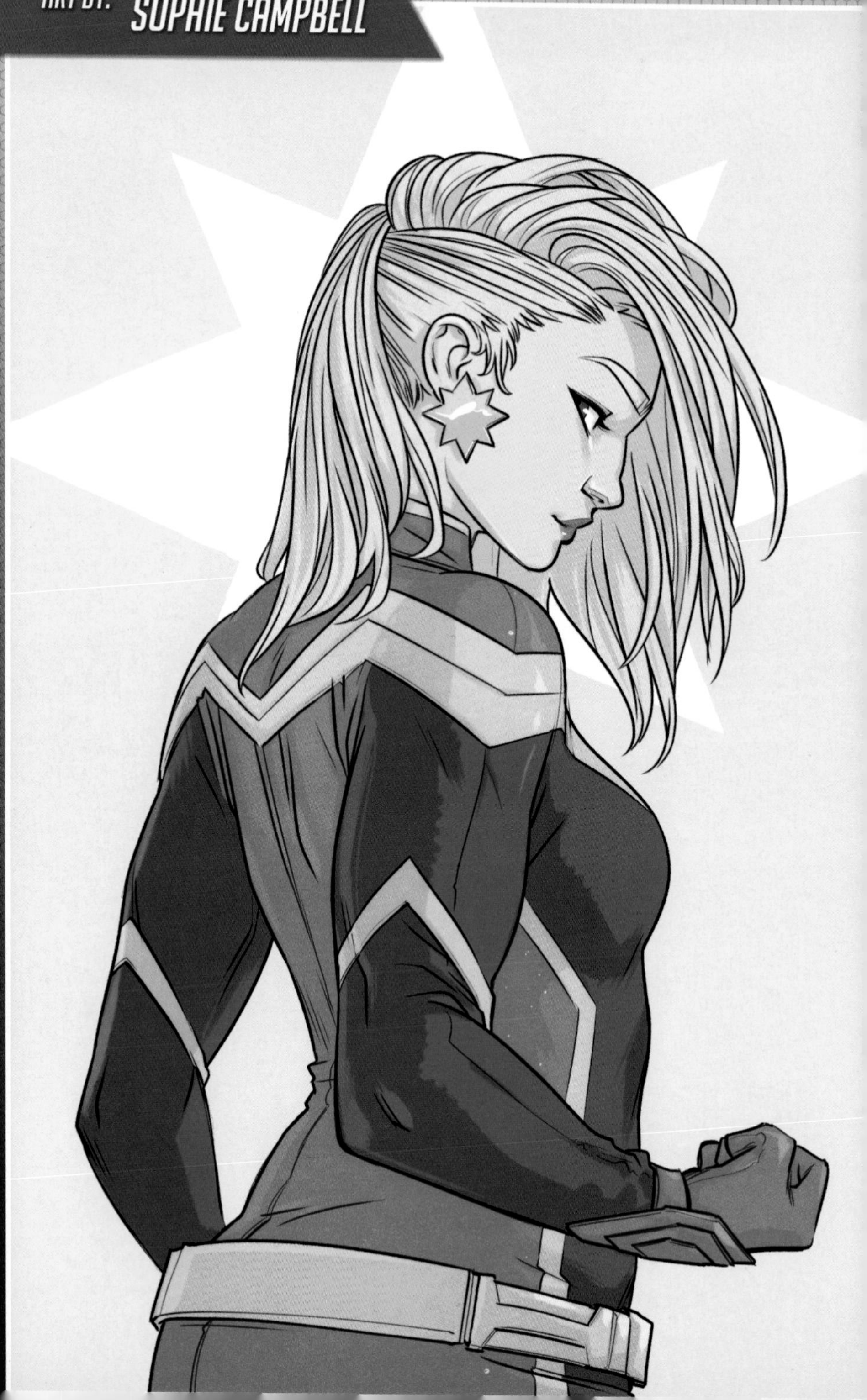

ART BY: GABRIEL RODRIGUEZ
COLORS BY: NELSON DANIEL

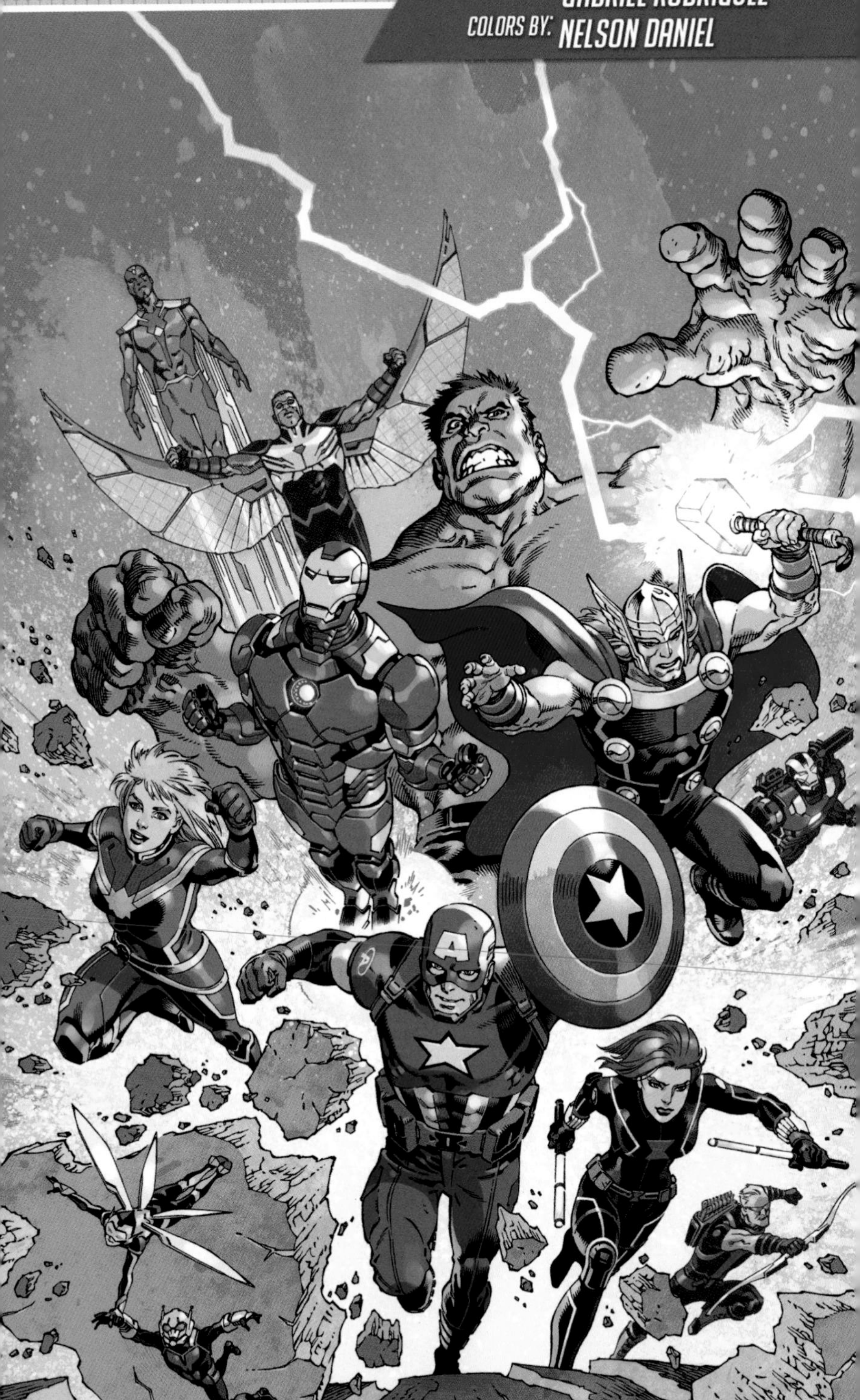